Peri

Indie Sparks

Twice Shy Publishing

Content Disclosure

Peri is a romance, but it is also a grief story. Grief can take many different paths, and we can find ourselves processing it in the aftermath of different types of mistakes or loss. I hope if you are dealing with any form or stage of grief, this story will be healing, or at the very least, will remind you that things get better. Grief does fade, and while life may never be the same, it can be good.

With all this said, I always want you to take care of yourself and be informed about what you will find in the pages of my books.

This book contains:
Parent loss in the current timeline.
Past parent loss.
Grief on the page.

It also contains:
Mature content, including consumption of alcohol, use of profanity, and detailed intimate scenes, including language that some readers may find crude or offensive. There are minor crimes committed and interaction with law enforcement (no violence exhibit-

ed by police officers). A secondary character experiences pregnancy and child birth.

EVERY SMALL-TOWN GIRL WITH A WILD STREAK WIDER
THAN MAIN STREET DESERVES:

The Best of Friends to Share in Her Antics
A Dirty Hometown Boy to be Her Partner in Crime
Parents Who Love Her, No Matter What

Some of those deserving girls never have any of those things. And
of those who do, most will lose at least one too soon.

There is no wrong time to be happy. It might not last, but whenever it finds you, you deserve it.
Be as wild as life allows, as dirty as you want, and as happy as you
can, always.

1

Bryce

I GLANCE UP FROM the rotisserie chicken display in time to see her walk through the automatic doors. She's been back in town for two weeks, and the first place I catch a glimpse of her is in the grocery store at nine o'clock on a Friday night. Figures.

I've broken my routine every night since she's been home, hoping she'd show up at Freeloaders' Bar, Salty's Barbecue, The Krazy Kactus . . . hell, I even met my sister at Jolene's Wine Bar.

Okay, I *invited* my sister to Jolene's. A fucking wine bar. I'll be listening to a ration of shit about that from my brother-in-law for the rest of my damn life. But that was it, my final attempt at accidentally running into her.

Could she have shown up at one of those places where I was cleaned up and ready to face her? No, of course not. Not Peri Abshire. She waltzes into the damn H-E-B looking red-carpet-ready when, truth be told, I'm not even clean enough to be in public.

I'm covered in sweat and sawdust from the shop, exhausted, and just trying to grab the quickest meal I can think of that's not fast food so I can eat, shower, and fall face-first into my bed. This is what I get for trying to cut back on cheeseburgers. If ever there was a night when I should've cared fuck-all about my health and hit a drive through, this is it.

Where'd she go?

That's what I get for trying to pretend I didn't see her by staring down at these overcooked yard birds. Like the choice between lemon-pepper and plain was going to matter to my stomach. I ate lunch early, and I'm starving right now. Or I was, anyway.

I should get out of here while I can make a smooth getaway. She probably didn't even notice me.

"Why are you mumbling at dead chickens?"

"Shit, Peri! Fuck. Damn." I run my hand through my hair and ignore the sawdust, falling like snow at my side. Great. The one day I go to the shop without a cap. I left it hanging on the hook right by my front door this morning because my mind was somewhere else, exactly where it's been for the last two weeks. It's a wonder I haven't sheared off a finger or two. My head's been fucked six ways from Sunday since the moment I heard she was back.

"I'll wait," she says, her wide eyes mapping my hair, which I know by the way she tilts her head is standing up all over.

I smooth my hair down, releasing less debris than before, but not none. "Wait for what?"

"You to finish reciting every cuss word in the English language, I guess. Is that not what you were doing?"

"I'm just trying to pick out one of these *dead chickens*, as you called them, for dinner."

"Well, they're not alive."

"That would make it harder to keep them in the little plastic containers."

"Oh, I don't know." She eyes the selection. "Once you had the lid closed, I bet the average chicken would probably just hunker down and wait for whatever came next. They're not very smart, even when they're not dead."

"When you're done ruining my appetite, maybe you could say hello."

"Hello, Bryce. Did you forget to pay your water bill?"

"I just got off work. Haven't made it home to shower yet."

"Is this how you look every day after work?"

"Is this how you look every time you come to the grocery store? Who are you trying to impress?"

She smiles, and I immediately wish she hadn't. I want her to be less beautiful, her lips to look less kissable, her skin less touchable, her body less . . . fuck, this is unfair. The eight years since we last saw each other have been more than kind to her. Not like I don't know she probably spends a fortune to look this good, but right now, all I can say is it's money well spent.

"Well, I'm not trying to impress these chickens," she says. "Because they're—"

"Dead." I finish the sentence with her, and we both laugh. Laughing with her over some stupid comment feels way too familiar. But we're not familiar anymore. We can't just pick up where we left off and start pulling pranks on each other again, or hiding from the cops after we graffitied the mural on the side of Crawford's Hardware or trespassing in the mayor's pool when we thought no one was home or any of the other dumb shit we did.

In our defense on the mural, you can't paint a giant pair of hands with the words "Here to help when you're getting handy" next to it and expect teenagers not to deface it. We weren't the only two involved in that one. The girl could paint an eye-catching giant dick, though. Just one of her many talents.

"Why are you at the grocery store this late at night?" I ask. "Hell, why are you here at all? Aren't there women from the church volunteering to do everything? I assumed for your mom they'd be falling all over themselves."

"Yes, there is an army of them. I needed to get out of the house for a while to breathe. I'm never alone. I appreciate the hospice nurses, but all the other visitors aren't helping as much as they'd like to believe. Not to mention, some of them are there just to see and be seen. They show up with the sun and stay until midnight. I'm about to bring the hammer down and create a visitation schedule."

"That should go over well."

She shrugs. "They all basically hate me already. The wayward daughter and all. Sammie Jo's mom pulled me aside the day after I got here to ask if I thought it was a good idea to wear my hair in a ponytail *after all that mess back when,* said some folks might think I was wearing my hair that way just to thumb my nose at the whole thing. So, now, I get up every morning and put my hair in a nose-thumbing ponytail just to show her rude ass exactly how much I care about upsetting people over something that happened eleven damn years ago."

"Of course, you do." I can't help but wince at knowing she's still having to listen to snide comments about that ponytail bandit shit. Jesus, we were kids. And I was an idiot. "No ponytail tonight though."

"No. I met Katie with a K at Jolene's. I gotta admit, I never thought this shithole town would turn into such a trendy little enclave. I might've come back sooner if I'd known." She laughs at that, but it's edged with more sarcasm than humor. There's only one thing that could've brought her home, and it's not a wine bar.

"You could've just said Katie and I'd have known which one you meant. Catie with a C is pregnant again, due any day."

"Damn, is Keller trying to field his own baseball team?"

"These days, I think he's pretty much just trying to keep chicken nuggets on the table."

"Y'all are still close, huh?"

"Yeah. Our lives couldn't look any different, but we still keep up with each other."

"That's good. I don't keep up with anybody from here anymore. I ran into Katie at the post office and she invited me to meet her at Jolene's to catch up. I can't bring alcohol into my mama's house, even though she'd never know at this point, and a few glasses of wine sounded really good."

"You all caught up now?"

"I think I might be. So, our biology teacher is *supposedly* a cryptocurrency billionaire, but everybody in town knows how he *really* made his money. Our algebra teacher is a trans woman who lives on some island somewhere. Lizzie's daddy will never be sheriff again after what happened with her brother's wife. Lizzie hasn't fully forgiven her dad or her ex-sister-in-law-now-stepmom, but she loves her little half-sister. Her brother has not yet found it in his heart to forgive anyone involved, but he moved to Chicago, so he doesn't have to see any of them anymore. Thankfully, he didn't have any kids with his cheating whore wife, so he was free to make a clean break. And the big blue Victorian over on Maple Street is some kind of porn studio? It's legal due to a loophole in the law, but there's a group of *concerned citizens* digging into how they can shut it down." She takes a breath. "Whew. Did she miss anything?"

"Did Katie with a K actually use the phrase trans woman?"

"To her credit, she actually did, but she never told me how Mr. Brannigan really made his money."

"Depends on who you ask. But the blue house on Maple is leased out to multiple businesses, one of which happens to be an artist who does nude photography."

"Well, clearly, nekked people are pornographic."

She says nekked with the most exaggerated Copper, Texas accent I've ever heard. But the way I want to get nekked with her right now might qualify as genuinely pornographic.

"Why are you looking at me like that, Bryce Callaway?"

This is Peri. If I hedge and go the gentleman route, she'll probably give me more shit for that than if I just come right out and say exactly what I'm thinking. She already knows. I can see the dare dancing in her eyes, but it might be only a dare for me to admit it. "Because I want to fuck you right here in front of these dead chickens, Peri Abshire."

"Well, after all these years, I would think you'd know I only fuck in front of live chickens."

"That can be arranged."

"You'd have to shower first."

"I can be quick."

"You better be talking about the shower."

Holy shit, is this really happening?

"You want to meet me at the house or ride with?"

"I'll drive myself."

I don't say another word, just turn and walk toward the exit, hoping like hell she's following me. When we approach the glass doors, and I see her reflection behind me, my dick jumps in my jeans, swelling against my zipper.

There is a better than average chance she's leading me on and fully plans to take the first cutoff back to her mom's place, but I've never backed down just because the odds weren't in my favor. Not when it came to Peri. Not when she looked at me with those fuck-me eyes and made me believe I had a shot. I always took my shot with her.

2

Peri

I ROLL MY WINDOW down a few inches as I take the last curve before Bryce's house, the same house he grew up in. I lower the window a few more inches. The air-conditioner works fine in my car, but I need all the air flow I can get right now.

This is a bad idea. At best, it's going to make me paranoid about running into him again, because this is definitely a one-time thing, but it's a thing I really, really want. At worst, I'll want to do it again. And that's not happening.

But my life is currently filled to the brim with wanting things that will never happen, so what's one more? I want my mom to get well. I want back all the time I lost. If I could do it all over, I'd come home more, wouldn't have left town again so fast after Daddy died. Eight fucking years gone in the blink of eye.

I'm barely staving off grief and she's not even gone yet. They say it can make people do things they wouldn't normally do, but I've read the books, and I know the warning signs; although frankly, they don't all sound terrible to me. The familiar becomes more attractive, even when it's not what's best for you. Not that Bryce has ever not been attractive. Goddamn, nobody has a right to look that good when they're tired and filthy. Maybe he's never been the best thing for me, but tonight, I know he's exactly what I need. Show me the harm in that.

I've barely left the house since I've been back, and it's only partially because I'm afraid she'll die and I won't be there. The other part has been my fear of running into Bryce, that I might see hatred in his eyes, or worse, indifference.

But when he looked at me tonight, I saw something else entirely, and I selfishly want to see it again. I want him to look at me like that because it's only ever felt good to be adored by his eyes. It still feels right after all these years, and if it's wrong, well, it won't be first wrong thing we've done together.

Seeing him in H-E-B was like stepping into a time machine, but one that took us all the way back to before it all went bad. When I walked in there, I sure wasn't looking for him, but there he was, and when we started talking, it felt like we were finishing an old conversation, one we'd left abruptly, which is exactly how we left each other.

Whatever else we do together tonight is going to end the same way. Clean break. Go our separate ways, but with no resentment this time. We're adults now, and we're going to be living in the same town again for a while. And I can't keep hiding in my house. Maybe we both need this.

Closure. I hate that word, but it feels appropriate. And I hate that more.

Bryce turns and drives through his gate. I slow down. For a flickering moment, I consider driving past it and going home, but I never felt anything other than safe and loved inside the walls of his house, and those things don't await me inside my childhood home, anymore. That house is filled with fear and uncertainty, and even though it's where I should be right now, I can't go back there yet.

The constant chatter of busybodied church ladies makes me angrier every day because my mom's the one dying instead of them. I'm not proud of feeling that way, but denying it doesn't make it any less true. I wish it was any one of them instead of her.

This is good, running into Bryce and following him home. Fate. I'll probably handle things better afterward, be kinder, less stressed. I turn onto his gravel drive. My headlights illuminate the vanity plate on his truck: C-WAY13.

I can't believe he still has his damn high school nickname on his plates. And his so-called lucky number. For all I know, people still call him C-Way. Hopefully, no one is still calling him *Three-Way C-Way*. I swear this town produces more idiots than most. Bryce Callaway was the golden boy, but even he wasn't having three-ways in high school.

I bet he's had a few since. He hasn't always lived here; he just came home sooner than I did. And more permanently.

Bryce opens his front door, and a dog comes barreling out. It's a mastiff, but it's too small to be Beans. This is a pup—a giant one, but still. I step out of my car and the huge puppy leaps off the porch and heads straight for me. "Beans is gone?"

"Two years now." Bryce whistles, and the new dog stops, but then he steals a few more steps in my direction. I close the gap between us to give him head scritches, which he takes as a greenlight to jump up and plow into my legs, nearly knocking me on my ass.

Bryce shakes his head. "I just got this lunatic a few months ago. Training's going great, as you can see."

"What's his name?"

"Crash. It's what he does best. Good job staying on your feet, by the way."

"Hi, Crash." I look up at the porch. "I was always pretty good at standing my ground."

"That you were."

Oh, damn. That panty-melting smile has only gotten hotter. And more effective. It's still contagious, too. He smiles, I smile.

"I'm going to grab a shower. I think the best I've got to offer for food is probably going to be ham sandwiches."

"Got any turkey?"

"Nope. Would've had chicken, but you ruined that plan."

I bite back a comment about how ruining each other's plans might be what we do best. "Maybe I'll just have cheese on mine."

"I do have cheese. Probably nothing as fancy as you're used to these days, but it says cheese on the package."

"Well, if it says it on the package . . ." I shove Crash, urging him toward the house. He stops to pee, an amount that has to be close to a gallon, before he races back through the front door, slipping on the rug and sliding a few feet. "I see what you mean about the name."

"He's not graceful, but he's happy."

"Happy's good." Crash gets back on his feet, and I pet him again. Bryce laughs at his clumsy dog, who's inching closer to me. The house looks different inside, but it feels the same. Best of all, it's calm—the air isn't thick with dread, no women in the kitchen spewing gossip like dueling fountains.

I kick off my heels and sink into his couch as he walks down the hall to shower, but I get right back up again. I'll fall asleep if I don't. There is too much peace and quiet here to prevent it.

The piano in the corner is still covered with family photos, but some have been removed. There are just as many frames as ever, but now they include a recent picture of Bryce with friends on a fishing boat, graduation pictures of his niece and nephew, who apparently both had the audacity to keep growing while I've been gone, a picture of him with Keller and Catie on their wedding day: the best man, his best friend, and the not-yet-showing pregnant bride. Who would've thought those two would stay together?

My fingers trace the silver rosettes around the edge of the largest frame, his parents' wedding photo. They really were great people. Life is so goddamn unfair.

His kitchen has been fully remodeled. It's nice, but it makes me a little sad not to see his mom's red stand mixer on the old beige Formica countertop, or her cherry-covered cafe curtains hanging over the sink.

Everything is new and modern: glass tile backsplash, brushed-nickel finish on the hardware and fixtures, teal stain on the cabinets, and polished concrete countertops. Almost sterile, but not. This is actually really pretty. He must've had a good designer. Or maybe a girlfriend at the time who gave him some input. Somebody convinced him to spend some money on these high-end appliances, that's for sure.

In his entire giant fridge, there is a cluster of condiment bottles that includes three mustard choices, barbecue sauce, and ranch dressing, half a stick of butter, a takeout container, a ripped open twelve-pack of beer with four cans left in it, a filtered-water pitcher, a bag of deli ham and a pack of American cheese—more accurately *pasteurized prepared cheese food product.* Yeah, no. The only way that's acceptable is in a grilled cheese.

I find a selection of nonstick pans, all new and very nice, in a lower cabinet, but that's not what I'm after. The real deal is in the next cabinet I open. Cast iron. These are definitely left over from his mom's kitchen. No wonder the others look unused. They were probably a gift, but I bet he only ever uses the cast iron. I pull out the largest skillet.

The loaf of bread in his pantry is marginally fresh, good enough for grilled cheese. I'm flipping the sandwiches when he steps into the kitchen, wearing nothing but a towel, his hair damp, and his pecs still glistening with water droplets he either missed or that dripped down from his hair after he dried off. *Oh, sweet familiar temptation, indeed . . .*

"Still not a shy bone in your body, obviously."

"You didn't have to do this," he says. "But it smells really good in here."

"I put ham in yours."

"Stop. You're going to make me come. The only thing that could make this moment better would be if you took your clothes off while you finished cooking them."

"Shut up and get me a beer." I slide the pan off the burner, and while he wrestles a couple cans from the twelve-pack, I slip the straps of my black jumpsuit off my shoulders, let it fall to the floor, and step out of it. I'm not entirely naked by the time he turns with the beers in his hands, but I'm down to my bra and panties. And they match. Black, lacy, and barely there.

He swallows, and his eyes roam down my body and back up again. The towel shifts over his hardening cock. I reach for a beer, and he places it in my hand. We pop our tops together, smile, and take our first sips at the same time.

I've already taken plates out and set them on the table. I set my beer on the counter and carry the skillet over to plate the sandwiches. Walking the pan back to the stove, I can feel the feral energy burning through his gaze.

This is what I'm here for, not to reminisce, not to cry on his shoulder, not to pretend we are the *us* we used to be. But he needs to eat dinner, and all I've had today is an apple and some pretzels, so food's a good idea all around.

I nod at the end of the table. "I assume you sit there." It's where I've placed the sandwich with ham in it.

"Right now, I'll sit wherever you tell me to."

"Keep being so cooperative and maybe I'll sit wherever you tell me to after we eat."

He walks to the table, picks up his sandwich, and takes a bite that wipes out nearly half of it.

I stand behind the chair and take a much smaller bite of mine, knowing I'm not going to get a chance to finish it before he pounces. We both wash our first bites down with another swig of beer while the air between us crackles with tension.

My hair slides across my shoulder and tickles my skin. When I shiver, it's game over for his restraint. The towel drops from his waist, and he sweeps my legs out from under me. I'm cradled in his arms and being kissed senseless as he carries me down the hallway toward his room, a room that used to be off limits because it belonged to his parents.

Being in this room instead of his childhood bedroom makes everything feel suddenly less familiar. This is the room of the man he is now, not the boy I knew then—not a stranger, but still someone new.

And I'm not sure if the stark reminder that I don't know him anymore makes this better or worse.

3

Bryce

As GOOD AS SHE looked wearing that black jumpsuit, nothing could've prepared me for the sight of her body when she took it off. Her underwear has damn sure gotten a lot sexier since the last time I saw it. All of her is a thousand times sexier now. This grown version of the girl I never got over is so different from the way I'd created her in my imagination, but so much the same as she ever was.

Her body in my arms still feels like it belongs there, her kiss still drives me wild, and she still radiates enough body heat to keep a man alive in a blizzard. Hottest girl in town always had more than one meaning when it came to her.

I let her feet find my bedroom floor, but not until we're standing next to the bed. Taking her face in my hands, I kiss her again. I need her to know how badly I want her right now, but also that I know what she's going through, and that it's okay if she needs to use me to escape the pain. We can do this however she wants. This time, anyway.

She reaches for the front-hook of her bra and opens it, letting the cups spread apart, but they still cling to her breasts. I pull the straps down her arms, and she lifts her shoulders to release the lace from her body. It falls to the floor, and I lower my head to kiss one of her hardened nipples, tracing with my tongue, sucking until she arches her back and threads her fingers into my hair. I move to the other and show it the same attention before squeezing her tits together, enjoying the soft weight of them, the perfect view of the swells spilling over my fingers, her nipples wet from my mouth.

My hands glide down her sides, mapping the curve of her waist and her hips, hooking my thumbs into the band of lace at the top of her panties and sliding them down her legs. I drop to my knees to take them to the floor, and help her step out of them, kissing my way back up her thighs, stopping to spread her pussy and drag my tongue through her seam.

The taste of her floods my tongue, and I could stay right here until she comes all over it, but I want her relaxed while I pleasure her, not worried about falling down. I tease a few circles around her clit before I stand and press on her shoulders to guide her to sit on the bed.

She reaches for my cock and my body quakes under her touch. I catch her shoulders to halt her when she slides forward. As much as I'd love to feel her warm mouth around my dick, I want her to come first, to remember that she always came first with me. I don't know how she's been treated since, but even as a boy, I got that much right. Older cousins can be a fount of knowledge. That last thing I want to do tonight is fall short of any good memories of me she has left.

"Lie back, beautiful. Let me take care of you."

The way her breath catches and her eyes glisten shows me how badly she needs to let go. She slides up until her head finds my pillows. I crawl onto the bed, and she lets her legs fall wider for me. Pressing my palms against the backs of her thighs, I lift her legs and spread them farther, diving down to playfully bury my face in her sweet snatch, growling against her like a starved bear. She laughs, and I can literally feel the tension releasing from her body.

Her spine softens against the mattress as I stop playing and begin to lick her tenderly, lapping up her arousal and letting it coat my tastebuds. When the tip of my tongue circles her opening, her hips lift slightly, encouraging me to probe her.

I look up to find her watching me. Sliding two fingers inside her while I maintain eye contact, I curl my fingertips to stroke her walls until I find the spot that makes her squirm. Her pussy tastes so damn good, and I want to eat her out properly, let the momentum build until my teeth are grazing her and she's gushing all over my mouth, but sweet Jesus, this woman needs an orgasm now.

I continue to finger her while my mouth goes back to her swollen clit, circling, flicking, and then drawing it between my lips to rhythmically suck on it, pausing intermittently to let my tongue lave around it, edging her just the slightest bit before I pull her over the finish line.

She fists the comforter when her walls start to quiver. Her pussy clenches around my fingers, and I can feel her thighs pulling together, threatening to close against the sides of my head. I suck harder without ceasing now. Her breathing becomes clipped shrieks and her back arches so much I have to chase her pussy to maintain contact. I hold on to her ass while her muscles contract, and keep holding her to guide her hips back down to the bed when everything relaxes.

Tears stream down her cheeks, but she's not actively crying. Her eyes lock onto mine. "Fuck me, Bryce. Please." She flips over, goes ass up, face down. "Make it hurt," she says, glancing at me over her shoulder.

In the pale lamplight, I can tell her eyes have turned brighter, and greener, the shade they always turned when she came or cried.

"So gorgeous." I let my splayed hand roam over her ass cheeks before I lift it and slap. She groans and bites her bottom lip. "Do you want me to leave my handprint on this pretty ass?"

"Yes."

Damn, this is way beyond where we left off eleven years ago. I spank her again, and my cock surges, hard and needy, but it can wait. Getting reacquainted with this woman will be worth it. "Do you have a safe word?"

"No. I just say stop if I don't like something."

"I want you to give me one, a word just for me. What's my word, Pear?" I don't mean to use my old nickname for her, but it's out of my mouth before I can stop it.

Even with one side of her face obscured by my pillows, I can see the radiant smile that overtakes her mouth, and I know she's come up with a word. Anticipation seizes my stomach because she could say anything right now. I honestly have no guess, but that smile that tells me it's not going to be something random.

"Zucchini."

Of course she did.

Nearly twelve years later, and that's the memory she pulls from. I'd smarted off to my dad and he'd made me cancel plans to spend the day floating the river with her and a group of our friends. I had to stay home and do chores, starting with weeding the garden, picking whatever was ripe. I plucked a zucchini that had a wasp on it. Partly from reflex, but mostly from being a pissed off seventeen-year-old boy, I threw that zucchini as hard as I could. It caught her on the cheek as she walked into the garden, hit her hard enough to black her eye. Cue all the teenage jokes from our friends about how I gave her a black eye with my zucchini. And the long talk with her dad to assure him I could control my temper around his daughter. I didn't know she was coming over. She wasn't supposed to be there, but I acted without thinking, regardless, lost my temper, just like he said.

Shame kept me from seeing any humor in it back then, but dammit, it is funny now. This is the first time I've ever been able to laugh about it. She's practically hysterical, so proud of herself for her witty safe word. "Okay, funny girl. Zucchini it is." I smack her ass again, harder than before, now that we've got an official safe word in place.

The pink handprint forming on her skin looks a hell of a lot better than that black eye did. My hand rubs over the stinging heat I've caused. She's not smiling anymore, but her eyes are still my favorite shade of green.

If I don't stop, she's going to have an ass covered in bruises because this is a game to her, a competition, and she's still as strong-willed as ever. I'll never hear the word zucchini come out of her mouth again tonight. I lean forward, press my lips to her ear and whisper, "zucchini."

"I didn't say it yet."

"I said it for you. You'll still have my handprint on your ass this time next week."

"Well, damn. That's going to interfere with my Playboy shoot."

"Good. My plan worked." I move her hair aside to kiss her neck. She writhes and my cock twitches. "You want to roll over or stay like this?"

"Stay like this."

I wonder if she wants it this way because it feels less intimate, but I don't press her. I'm more than happy to fuck her while I look at my handprint all over her ass. Going up onto my knees, I guide the swollen head of my dick through her slick seam a few times to coat it with her juices. *Fuck, what am I thinking?* "I've got condoms in the nightstand."

"Don't," she says. "Tell me you're clean, and I'll trust you."

"I am."

"Me, too. I understand if you'd feel safer—"

I push forward, sinking the tip inside her before she can finish her sentence. "The last woman I fucked bare was you."

"Same. I mean—"

"I know what you mean." I slide the rest of my cock into her tight pussy. The way my body shudders in response to her blissful heat shakes the bed, and her gasp is everything.

Gripping her hips with both hands, I slam into her. This is raw lust, the kind that can't be held back, and I don't think she wants me to do that, anyway, so I fuck her with unbridled force. Round one was always going to be quick. I've wanted to be back inside her for too damn long.

4

Peri

BRYCE'S BREATHING STEADIES, GETS deeper, and I'm pretty sure he's asleep. My head is on his chest, but he's been quiet for a good five minutes now. I try to roll out of his embrace, and his hand immediately slides between my legs. "I don't know where you think you're going. You've only had one orgasm." "Yeah, well, one's going to have to do it. I need to get home."

"No. Don't go, Peri. Stay with me. She has an overnight nurse, right?"

"An overnight nurse, plus at least two women from the church until at least midnight. And I need to get back there, too, to face their judgmental stares as I slink in the door." I laugh, but the truth is I haven't been away from the house this long, and I'm getting anxious. "I really have to go, Bryce."

"I know. I'm sorry for being selfish." He nods at the tent his dick has pitched in the comforter. "Blame him."

"I'm glad I ran into you tonight. I think we needed this."

"I guarantee I did." He sits up and swings his legs over the side of the bed. "I'll walk you out."

"You don't have to do that." I've got my bra and panties back on already. "My jumpsuit is still on your kitchen floor, and my shoes are in the living room. I'll finish getting dressed on my way out."

He stands and zips the jeans he's pulled on. "And then I'll walk you out."

"Okay, yes, you can walk me out."

"It was never a question."

I shimmy back into my jumpsuit in the middle of his kitchen, and he wraps his arms around me from behind. "I could watch you take this off and put it back on all day, every day."

An uneasiness burns in my core. I pull away from him and go to the living room. He's not going to see me do either of those things again. This was a one-night stand. Sort of. Same principle. I wiggle my foot into my shoe, bend my knee to kick up my heel, and reach down to fix the strap. Crash sits on top of my other shoe and waits for me to pet him before he'll budge. With both shoes finally on, I lead the way through Bryce's front door.

When I yank open my car door and try to hop inside, he grabs my arm and pulls me back. "You can't possibly think this is how things are going to go now." His mouth crushes mine in a punishing kiss. I resist kissing him back, but only for so long because I'm not made of stone. "I'm not done with you."

"You are for tonight." Why'd I say that? That makes it sound like I'm willing to sneak over here again.

"What are you doing tomorrow night?"

"Staying home, like I should've done tonight."

"Do you really think that's what you should've done?"

"I don't mean that I feel guilty about what we did, but I should be there, with her. Everything is just really hard right now."

"Huh. Some people might think I'd understand exactly how fucking hard things are for you right now, given that I've been through it already."

"Shit, I'm sorry. I forget. I don't mean I forget that she's gone. I loved your mom, too, Bryce. And I'm sorry I wasn't here to say goodbye to her. I'm sorry I didn't come for the funeral." I stare at the ground and blink back tears. "I couldn't. There's no excuse for it, but I just couldn't."

"I know. And I'll never forgive myself for being the reason you wouldn't come home, but you're here now, and there is so much I want to say to you. Don't run from me again, Pear. Please."

That's the second time tonight he's called me Pear, and it hurts to hear it come out of his mouth. The soft way he says it, the way I want to be that girl with him again. But that girl finally grew up. And so did he. We didn't do it together; we never could've done it together. "I've got to go."

He steps back and let's me get in my car, watches me drive away. Crash chases my tires until I pull out of the gate. I slow to make sure he runs back to the house. "Good boy."

5

Bryce

CRASH LIVES UP TO his name thirty minutes before sunrise, careening into the side of my bed to pant in my face with his hot dog breath.

I make coffee while Crash eats his morning snacks, and remind myself I only have two more Saturdays in the shop. I got a big contract to do custom cabinetry for three jewelry store remodels. The owner wanted all custom and everything to match. I'm so close to being done. After that, I'll have my full weekends back for a while. My sister calls, as if on cue to bitch at me about working too much, among other things.

"I didn't get myself in a bind, Lisa. It's a pretty damn great position to be in. Hell, I honestly didn't expect to get this job when I bid it. I got lucky, and the job's almost done. I'm not even doing the install at his stores. He's having his general contractor pick them up from the shop."

I watch Crash roll in something in the yard while I lean on the railing of my deck, drinking coffee and listening to my sister tell me how my nephew isn't taking school seriously enough. Lisa is the stereotypical, overachieving first-born child, never stepped out of line, never broke a rule, so when her kids act like kids, she panics. She's been saying her son acts just like me since he hit puberty. I wear that shit like a badge of honor, but I can't tell my sister that.

"He's a college freshman," I say, "and he's acting like one. If he messes up, he'll learn from it. He's a good kid, but it's his first time out of the house. He'll figure it out."

I make a mental note to call him and ride his ass about not fucking up, but I'm not going to tell her I plan on doing it. I intervene behind the scenes every now and then, because he does act an awful lot like me sometimes. I understand him in ways she doesn't, but I promised him a long time ago he could count on me, and that I wouldn't tell his mom things he doesn't want her to know. Or his dad, and weirdly, that one's harder. So far, the kid hasn't made me break that promise, but it never hurts to check in with him to be sure he's not going off the rails.

After making it clear I've been absolutely no help regarding what to do about my nephew, she says, "So, have you seen her yet?"

"Yeah. We ran into each other last night."

"Wow, she finally got out of that house. Good. Where'd you see her?"

"Grocery store."

"That's more boring than I was hoping for. Did you talk?"

"We did."

"How is she?"

"As good as could be expected."

"Did you ask her to have dinner with you? Lunch? Brunch? Anything? If you want to talk to her, you have to let her know, Bryce."

"She knows."

Lisa sighs like I'm as big a pain in her ass as my nephew. "You're not going to give me any details, are you?"

"Not at this juncture, no." I whistle for Crash. He makes it halfway back before he trips over his front paws.

"Did you at least tell her it was good to see her or compliment her or make sure she knows you're here for her if she needs anything? Did you do anything to let her know you still care?"

I left my handprint on her ass. How many points would you give me for that? "Yes, I was kind, considerate, and my usual charming self."

"Oh, God. I wish I'd been there to help you." She sighs again. "Hopefully, you weren't too aloof."

"I was no amount of aloof, trust me."

"Bryce . . . you know she's in a vulnerable place right now. Tell me you didn't do anything stupid."

"Love you. Gotta go." I end the call.

I need work today, something to focus on other than Peri.

6

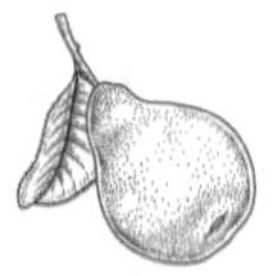

Peri

I SNEAK IN THROUGH the front door of my own house, knowing the women who've taken up residence will probably all be in the kitchen.

Wrong! They're holding court in the living room today, and I walk right into a circle of side-eyes and grimaces. All I did was run out to grab a to-go coffee because they commandeer the damn coffee maker at the crack of dawn and fill it with coffee-flavored water. I need jet fuel in my cup, but I was only gone twenty minutes, max. Slinking in after midnight last night didn't go unnoticed either. But that's exactly why I need the caffeine.

Raising my paper cup in salute, I walk past them. I don't make it three steps before the voices come for me.

"Again with the ponytail?"

"And a ballcap today to boot."

"Is courting controversy really so important at a time like this, Peri?"

I squeeze my cup until the lid pops off. It's the perfect physical metaphor for what's happening in my head right now. "Shut your fucking mouths." I round to face them all. "You want to know what's uncalled for at a time like this? Your snide comments that would upset my mother as she lays dying. They've upset me for the last goddamn time. Do you hear me? You better listen because I'm only going to say this once. If you insist on being here, you will keep your shitty comments to yourselves from now on, or I will kick every one of you out of here so fast it makes your clumped-up mascara run down your powder-caked faces. Are we clear?"

A few of the women nod, keeping their lips tight. But there's always one that just can't keep her mouth shut. Today, that one is Jeannie Watts.

"Can you at least not go around wearing a ballcap? I'm sorry, but you're just begging people to dredge up that ponytail bandit nickname again. It's not like it wasn't clear how much you loved the attention back then."

"Did I, Jeannie? Did I love being interrogated by the police as a terrified seventeen-year-old, being told the FBI could be next? Did I love watching adults whispering about me everywhere I went? How about the last few months of high school? How do you think that felt? And that scholarship I lost because people just couldn't stop posting every article on social media and tagging me in it? Do you think I loved that, too? How about the comments people left on those posts, detailing every bad thing I'd ever done, and a whole slew of shit I never even thought of! Maybe I deserved all that, huh? Is that what you think?"

"Well, if you'd ever once apologized, it might've—"

"For what? I didn't do it! Hot tip, search the phrase *ponytail bandit and bank robbery* and see how many results you get from all over the country. People love to think they're more creative than they are, but it really wasn't such a clever nickname. The woman in the bank's surveillance video was clearly heavier than me, taller than me, but when someone anonymously turns in your name, you get investigated, regardless.

"I was cleared as a suspect, but there was no going back. I couldn't erase it, undo all the hurtful things people said to me, to my parents, who y'all claimed to care so much about. The whole trajectory of my life got changed, and you still think I should be afraid to wear a damn ballcap and a ponytail? Fuck. You."

A collective gasp sucks the oxygen from the room.

"Well, honey, I hate to say it, but you had such a reputation by that point. You were just running wild. Every time your poor mama turned around, you were in trouble for something new. Can you really blame anyone for being suspicious? And people can't help but think it's strange that, to this day, no one else has been arrested for it."

"The statute of limitations is long over, Jeannie. It's time to let it go, but you can do it somewhere else. Get out. And don't even think about coming back."

She snatches her purse off the coffee table in a huff and stomps out. I eye the rest of them, waiting to see if anyone has anything to add. Without hesitation, Sandy Lindsey says, "If you ask me, I still think it's a little too coincidental that Bryce Callaway came forward and admitted he was the one who turned you in. I dare anybody to put a ponytail wig on that boy and look at that security footage again and tell me I'm wrong. That family has always thought they were better than everybody else, and they sure had the money and the connections to protect their precious boy."

I set my coffee on the console table under the TV and clap. "Brav-o, Sandy. That is one hell of a conspiracy theory. You have officially outdone yourself, you batshit crazy bitch. You can get the fuck out, too."

She opens her mouth to argue, but I lift my hand as a final warning for her to shut up. The nurse on duty comes down the hall, shushing me, but then she turns to the remaining women and says, "Whoever she's telling to get out should go. This is not the place for arguing. It's not my house, but that is my patient down that hallway." The nurse turns to me as if seeking my approval.

"She's right. And from now on, there will be no arguing, no gossiping, no negative words of any kind in this house. My mother has been good to every one of you, and you will be good while you're here or you will be told to leave. And whether the order comes from me or a nurse, it stands, and you will comply without question. This is still a home, not a community center for bored housewives."

I secure the lid back on my coffee and go to my room to drink it alone. Five more stolen minutes before I sit with my mom, my regrets, and the questions that will never have answers. But I'll wear this motherfucking ballcap and ponytail while I do it.

7

Bryce

"You really didn't ask for her number?" Keller laughs over the top of his beer. "Only you, man. Only you."

"It's Peri. Having to ask for her number didn't even cross my mind. I guess I assumed I'd see her again naturally."

"Like, where? Tomorrow at school?" He laughs harder. "Maybe if you hang out in H-E-B long enough—"

"Fuck you, asshole." I take a drink. "I think Katie with a K probably has it. They had to coordinate meeting at Jolene's somehow."

"And you want me to ask my wife, Catie with a C, if she could maybe call her up and get it for you."

"Yeah, but don't make it obvious it's for me."

"Oh, sure. I'll just tell my very pregnant wife that I'd like her to try to get Peri's number for me with no further explanation. Dude, I love you, but not that much."

"Okay, fine. Tell your wife how pathetic I am. It's been a week, Kell. She hasn't been on social media at all."

"You stalk her socials? That's cute."

"How many times do I have to call you an asshole in one day?"

"Relax. I'll do your dirty work. I need to get home, anyway. I'm the official bath giver right now."

"Just line them up in the backyard and spray them with the hose. Kids love shit like that. You'll be the cool parent."

"Yeah, marriage and fatherhood aren't going to hold any shocks for you at all."

"Tell Catie I appreciate her help. And tell her I said hurry up and have that baby."

"They say later babies come earlier. Leave it to our fourth to be a week late and still hanging out like she's on island time."

"The only girl. She's getting an early start on being late."

"Just like her mom." He tips his beer back to finish it off. "I'll let you know if I get Peri's number for you."

"I appreciate you."

"You should."

I like when Keller stops by my shop on his way home. He does it less often with every new kid they have, but seeing his truck pull in always makes me want to stop working and drink a beer, talk for a while. My mood's always a little lighter when he leaves.

As soon as I walk toward the garage doors to start closing up the shop, a car pulls in . . . Peri's car.

Damn, even Keller doesn't work that fast. I guess I didn't need her number after all. My chest tightens as I watch her step out of her car, and I send up a quick plea that she's not here because her mom's gone. I know it's coming soon, but she deserves more time with her.

She waves, walks around to her passenger side, and pulls out two grocery bags, holding them up as if they explain her presence.

"If you'd told me you were going to H-E-B, I'd have dirtied myself up a bit more and come right over."

Her laughter gets Crash's attention, and he abandons his butterfly chase to make a run for her knees. "Not today, buddy." She outruns him into the shop and drops the bags onto a work table. "I figured I still owed you a rotisserie chicken. I got some premade mac-and-cheese and some mashed potatoes to go with it. Cookies, too."

"Wow, nothing green. Impressive."

"It's not a green food kind of day." She takes two plastic forks from the bag and hands me one. "I didn't bother with paper plates. Figured we could just eat out of the containers."

"I'd have taken you to dinner, you know."

"I can't be seen in pubic with you. From what I hear, you might be a bank robber. In fact, I hear if we put a ponytail wig and a pink ballcap on you and compared it to the figure from that old Copper Bank and Trust security footage—"

"Goddammit. Sandy Lindsey's back on that bullshit again?"

"Wait. You know she thinks that about you?"

"I don't believe for a minute she really thinks it was me. I think that woman needs attention, and she's running out of ways to get it."

"Yeah, well, she's not getting it at my mom's house anymore. I kicked her out."

"Good for you. Wish I could've been there to see it."

"I kicked Jeannie Watts out, too."

"Damn. Clean house, girl."

"It's been an eventful week." She pops the domed lid off the chicken and peels back the skin before she rips off a piece and takes a bite. "So far, the rest of them are behaving, but I'll kick out the next one that gives me a reason."

I hop up onto the work table and try not to stare at her, but it's hard to look away. She's angry, and she'd punch me if I said it, but she's even prettier when she's pissed off. She always was. It's that fire in her eyes. I dig into the mashed potatoes while she takes the first bite of the mac-and-cheese.

"How's she doing?"

"She's dying. How the fuck do you think she's doing?" She takes a deep breath, lets it out slowly. "I'm sorry. You didn't deserve that. She's only awake for maybe a few hours a day total. Sometimes, she's lucid enough to smile and nod in response to a comment like she understands, but other times, she's just in and out, or wailing from the pain. They got the okay to increase her pain meds this morning, so those lucid moments are probably gone."

"I remember that stage. A blessing and a curse."

"Yeah, pretty much."

We continue to pull the chicken apart, trade the containers of mashed potatoes and mac-and-cheese every few bites until she finally speaks again. "So, I guess it won't be long now. I mean, the nurses said as much, but they can't say how long, maybe days, maybe weeks. I've never wanted a firm answer to anything more in my life. But maybe I don't. It just doesn't feel real."

"It won't for a while."

"And then all at once, it will?"

I swallow hard, wish I could sugarcoat the truth, but that's not what she needs. "Reality will hit, maybe all at once."

"I know. In my head, I know, but . . ." She shrugs because she doesn't have the words.

I nod to let her know I get it. She doesn't have to finish that sentence.

We eat a little more, talk a lot less. "You want a beer?"

"I don't think so. I meant to grab a bottle of wine, but I forgot."

"That is the one thing I don't have. But I know this trendy little wine bar every woman our age seems to love, which probably means we'd run into a few of them if we went there, and I bet they'd all be shocked to see the two of us walk in together."

"Two suspected bank robbers walk into a wine bar . . ." She smiles.

I laugh. "Let's give them something to talk about. Something more recent, anyway."

"Their gossip could definitely use an update."

"Follow me to the house. I'll grab a quick shower, and then we'll go reclaim our rightful place as the king and queen of scandalous behavior."

"I don't know what you think we're going to do in Jolene's, but you might need to scale back your expectations."

"We'll see." My wink gets another laugh out of her.

8

Peri

BRYCE'S EXPRESSION FALLS WHEN I tell him I'm taking my own car to Jolene's, and that I can only stay for one glass. As much as I needed to get out of the house, I can't be gone long or my anxiety spins out of control. It's impossible to balance the need to escape with the need to be there constantly. The only people who get it are the ones who've been through it, and I feel guilty talking to Bryce about it because it's not fair to put him through it all over again. I know he'll let me; I just don't know if it's right. Or what kind of confusion it could lead to. Everything beyond the current moment is incomprehensible, light years away.

We park next to each other in the lot between Jolene's and Crawford's Hardware. "I can't believe the mural is gone," I say. "It was iconic."

"New owners. They kept the name, but got tired of having to have the mural repainted every six months." He points up to the edge of the building. "Even after they installed the cameras, kids still found a way to disguise themselves and spray a quick obscene embellishment."

"I love that." I stick my tongue out at the blank brick wall. "Way to piss on tradition, new owners."

Bryce rests his hand at the small of my back when we walk in. The handy mural on Crawford's is gone but there's a giant mural of Dolly Parton behind the bar. It's done in neon paints, and it feels weirdly reassuring to see Dolly smiling at us so vividly.

I should've known better than to let my guard down though. "Oh. My. God. Alert the media!" Katie with a K shouts from across the room, because of course, she's here again. "Look who's together again!"

Bryce whispers, "Ten bucks says she calls us team toxic with the next words out of her mouth."

"Not Katie. I'm pretty sure she's still holding out hope she'll get to be co-maid-of-honor in our wedding."

She's walking toward us, motioning for us to come her way. "Come sit with everybody."

Everybody is a bold word to describe the three women avoiding their kids and husbands in an electric blue, velvet booth while knocking back sparkling wine. Who else could possibly exist beyond them? But how do we get out of it? If we decline the invitation and sit at the bar, it'll be all over town by tomorrow afternoon that I've moved back for good and am planning to marry Bryce. Or that we've eloped already.

It's a huge horseshoe-shaped booth, so we can't use lack of seating space as an excuse. I slide in first and give Bryce the end, the easiest exit spot. Of course, we know *everybody*. The hellos are awkward as hell. I definitely need a glass of cab, STAT. Bryce offers to go to the bar and takes *everybody's* order before he does, leaving me alone with them.

As soon as he's left, Katie says, "Hey, Peri, do you see what I see?" She nods toward the small stage at the back of the room. I'd seen it last Friday. Does she not remember we were here together?

Now I see what she's really talking about. It's a karaoke machine that I hadn't seen on my first visit. We were early last week, too. It probably gets a lot more use later in the night. "They've got y'all's song," she says.

"No. My karaoke days are over."

"Aw, come on. Your duet partner's here and everything." *Everybody* laughs and starts trying to convince me we have to do it. For old time's sake. As if I do anything for the sake of that these days.

Katie's memory is clear about Bryce and me being karaoke duet partners back in the day. And we did have a song: Islands in the Stream, but we modified some of the lyrics into a very NSFC (not safe for Copper) version, complete with grinding on each other and obscene hand gestures that got us a less-than-polite invitation to vacate the premises at more than one establishment.

"I'm too old to get kicked out of a wine bar."

"Oh, bullshit. Peri Abshire will never be too old to get kicked out of anywhere, let alone a bar." Katie declares.

The others goad her with their enthusiastic chant. "Do it. Do it. Do it."

Katie jumps up and runs over to the machine to cue up the song. She's wasting her time, making a fool of herself. My eyes catch Bryce walking back from the bar with another bottle of bubbles for *everybody* tucked under his arm, and a glass of cab for us in each hand.

The first notes play, and his wicked smile has me shaking my head in an emphatic NO. His waggles his eyebrows, and *everybody* hoots and hollers like he's started to strip. He sets the bottle and the glasses on the table and extends his hand.

"You can't be serious."

He gyrates his pelvis and sings, "You can ride it forever, ah ha."

Everybody falls like dominos, swooning and cracking up. The next thing I know, there is a force shoving on my shoulder and pushing me to the edge of the booth.

Bryce snatches my hand and yanks me up. I steal a gulp of my wine before he pulls me to the stage.

Jesus, fuck and then some. I can't believe I'm about to do this.

Bryce turns on a microphone and forces it into my hand before he takes the second one just in time to defile the opening lyric. "Baby when I met you, you were a piece unknown. I set out to get you with this big hard bone." He punctuates the last three words with perfectly timed pelvic thrusts.

Everybody whistles and catcalls. They're not the only people in here, but unfortunately, there is laughter rising from other tables as well. I have no ally here, not one. All these filthy animals are onboard for this.

It's natural to make fun of songs your parents like when you're a teenager, but I actually always loved this one. Our rendition was a crowd pleaser, though, and I did like the spotlight, especially when I could share it with Bryce. I join in with him, and before I know it, I'm backing my ass against his crotch as we croon our version of the chorus: "Horny and full of cream, we'll fuck in a car . . ."

The last few verses are harder to sing now. We could only dirty up so much with any hope of remaining on stage, so we mostly stayed true to those desperately sincere lyrics about staying togeth-er. But back then, we were young and wildly in love, and those words felt true. Tonight, I can't look him in the eye because they stir emotions I've managed to keep at bay for so long.

I pull out all the stops when we make it back to the chorus and give the crowd the vulgar finish they want. He juts his leg out for me to ride his thigh, and I don't hesitate to hop on. We used to end the performance with me flashing him with my back to the crowd. That's not on my agenda for this encore—until we're there, and I do it, pulling my top up and tossing my head back like I always did.

We get a standing ovation, and not one request to leave. I look to the bar and mouth an apology to Dolly as we leave the stage.

Everybody is still on their feet, but they slide back into the booth when we approach the table. I know without question that at least one of them videoed the performance, and we'll be all over social media within the hour. Anyone who didn't know I was back in town before will now.

Well, Bryce said we should give the wagging tongues of Copper something to talk about. We just lit the torch in the gossip Olympics. Let the games begin, I guess.

9

Bryce

I PULL THE GARAGE doors down on my last Saturday in the shop for a while. These cabinets will be on their way Monday morning, and I'll be on to my next project, which is much closer to my usual order. This one's been a challenge, and there were times I wasn't sure I'd get it done, even with the two guys I hired, but we did it.

"If y'all don't have to take off right away, you're welcome to grab a beer." I nod toward the fridge and they both smile and head in that direction.

The sound of Keller's truck pulls my attention. I reopen one of the doors and watch him kill the engine and hop out, wearing a smile from ear to ear that could only mean one thing.

"I assume congratulations are in order?"

"She finally decided to make her debut. I'm headed to Catie's parents' to show the boys pictures and eat dinner with them before I head back to the hospital."

"Catie and the baby are both good?"

"Doing great."

"Beer?"

"No. My father-in-law's probably got one waiting for me. I can't stay." He runs his hand through his hair. "I've got four kids now. Me! Can you believe this shit?"

"I might be the only person more shocked than you. You ever going to reveal this kid's name?"

"Isabella Peri."

"Wow."

"Catie always said Peri was the strongest, bravest girl she ever knew, and if she had a daughter, she was going to use the name. They were really close at one point."

"Yeah, they were."

"We're going to call her Bella, but it was important to Catie that Peri be her middle name. You don't think she'll be upset, do you?"

"No. If anything, I think she'll be honored. She and Catie drifted after she left, but their friendship didn't end in a fight. Peri dislikes a lot about this place, some of the people included, but not Catie."

"Sounds like you still know her pretty well."

"I'm sure there's plenty of new stuff I don't know about her."

"You could learn." He tilts his head and gives me a half-shrug. "Just saying. She's here. Might as well make the most of it."

"We sang Islands in the Stream in Jolene's last night."

"No shit?" He laughs—at me, not with me, I'm well aware. "I hope somebody videoed that."

"Katie with a K was front and center."

"Oh, cool. It should be easy enough to find then."

"Get out of here. Go show those little boys their baby sister."

We shake hands, and I pull him in for a hug. Before he drives away, he stares at me through his windshield and gives me the raised-eyebrow-half-shrug again, as if I need any more encouragement. His eyes are bloodshot, and I know he's exhausted, but he's still smiling.

I drink a beer with my guys. They've both got stories to tell and jokes to share, but she's all I can think about.

10

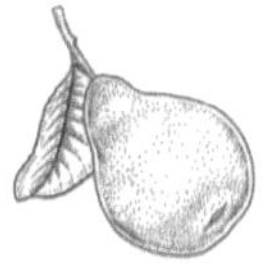

Peri

THE PANG OF REGRET I felt when Bryce texted earlier to ask if he could take me to dinner, and I turned him down, is how I know it was the right choice. Staying here tonight was already my plan, but when that moment of doubt, that brief hesitation to tell him no made me pause and reconsider, I knew for sure I needed to pump the brakes.

I catch a glimpse of myself in the mirror as I change into pajamas, and I turn to confirm all the bruising has completely faded. It's probably been gone for days, but I hadn't thought about it. My first thought when I look at my body now is how much I'd like to feel his hand on my ass again, both his hands on all of me.

It's not hard to figure out that the appeal is distraction, or part of it is, anyway. What's here is hard, but I can't run away from it. I don't want to abandon my mom; I want to be able to blink and reset everything. What we want isn't always possible, of course.

She can't ever seem to get warm enough, so we keep a heater going in her room. I pull on sleep shorts and a tank top to make it bearable, but I'd sit with her tonight if it was a hundred degrees in there.

The evening nurse just left. There's no point in having someone here overnight since I'm home, and she's on so much pain medication now it's like she's sedated, anyway. But I believe she can still hear me.

I push the recliner close to the edge of her bed and sit with my legs crisscross as I sip my iced tea and watch her sleep. I've got a book to read, another full of word searches and crosswords, and the TV remote in my lap, but I don't want any of those yet. She flinches without waking, and I reach for her hand.

"It's okay, Mama, just a dream." My voice sounds certain, but I'm more hopeful than sure. More than anything, I just don't want her to be in pain. She settles. Whatever it was has passed. "I'm going to be right here, okay? I've been gone a little more than usual the past couple of weeks. When I came in to tell you I was going out to run an errand, it wasn't always true."

A chill spreads over my exposed skin, but I know it's nerves more than the temperature of the room. I pull a blanket over my lap. "I've seen Bryce a few times. I know you still hold a grudge for what he did. You were always ready to fight a bear if you thought I'd been wronged, but the truth is, I forgave him a long time ago. We were kids. And I have a good life. I like my job and where I live. He didn't wreck my future, I promise. Going to a different college wasn't the end of the world. Leaving some friends behind probably wasn't the worst thing for me either." I laugh softly.

"I have another confession. I kicked Jeannie Watts out of your house. Sandy Lindsey, too. They just said the most hateful things, like I was trying to be a disgrace with every choice I made. You were always too nice to them, Mama. I'm sorry, but it's true. I know you told them about all the mother-daughter trips we took, but they acted like I just left and never saw you again. So what if I never came back here? You understood, and that's all that ever mattered to me."

I adjust my blanket and take a breath, center myself and try to let go of the negative stuff because whether it matters now or not, I know how easily I can still get defensive and caught up in the drama of it all.

"We went to some pretty great places together, didn't we? I'm so glad we saw the Joshua trees together, the desert in bloom, and nothing will ever top our weekends at the beach, shopping and laughing. But I guess there was a lot we never talked about, even in those beautiful places.

"You never pried into my life, and I probably didn't share nearly enough, but I always knew how much you loved me. I tell everyone I know that I have the best, fiercest, most loyal mom in the whole world. I have always known I was lucky to have you. I'm not leaving your side again, okay? I'm staying with you.

"But I might see Bryce again before I leave. I know me, but I'd forgotten the me I am when I'm with him, and maybe it's just nostalgia, but I think that might be the best version of me. We've both grown up. He never settled down with anybody else either. Maybe we wouldn't be bad for each other anymore. If you could, you'd probably tell me not to get ahead of myself. I don't want to stay in Copper, and he has his business here. Not to mention, we don't even really know each other as adults. I'm confused. And scared. Most of all, I don't want you to be disappointed in me. I never want to disappoint you again, Mama."

With my free hand, I wipe away the tears that have escaped and are slipping over my cheekbones. She presses her fingers against my other hand still holding hers.

"I felt that. Can you do it again?" She does. It's not a hard squeeze, but it's real. I know it is. "I love you, too."

My voice is a whisper when I tell her, "He still calls me Pear," as I lean back and untangle my legs. Exhaustion rolls over me like a wave, pulling me under.

Her hand slips from mine and I lunge forward to check on her. She's the same. I'd dozed off and let go of her, but I'm wide awake now. I open my crossword book.

"What's a seven-letter word for an idealized scenario?"

She wouldn't tell me if she was as wide awake as I am. She'd give me a hint. That's how she always helped, by giving suggestions or asking questions to make me think harder, so I could figure it out for myself, but never solving it for me.

I fill in the two words that bisect the one I can't get, and then I see it: *fantasy*.

11

Bryce

IT'S WAY TOO BRIGHT in my room when I roll over Sunday morning. Crash got me up twice last night to let him out. That's what I get for giving him his own slice of pizza. He begs. I'm weak.

I reach for my phone to check the time. Holy shit. I haven't slept past nine in years. There must be some frequency emitted when a phone screen wakes up that only dogs can hear. Crash tumbles at the end of the hallway and slides the rest of the way into my room.

"What have you been doing?" I ask. "There better not be trash all over my kitchen floor."

He hangs his head. Great. My phone screen lights up again.

I'm half laughing when I answer it. "Shouldn't you be changing a diaper?"

"Hey, man." Keller's voice is way too fucking somber.

I sit straight up. "Are Catie and the baby okay?"

"Yeah, yeah, they're both doing great. But Peri's mom died. Last night or early this morning, I'm not sure, but she's gone."

"Fuck. I'm headed over there." I drop the phone onto my bed, and take two steps toward my closet before I realize I didn't end the call. "Thanks for letting me know," I sputter before I end the call and drop the phone again. I don't even know if he was still on the line to hear me. All I know is I need to get to her house.

I fling the back door open and usher Crash out. "You gotta go now, buddy. I don't know how long I'll be gone."

My brain is spinning. What can I take her that would help? All I can think of is coffee or breakfast, but I know she won't eat. And there are probably already a dozen women there spreading food across the table and stuffing the fridge.

The edge of my bathroom sink is cold under my hands as I grip it to steady myself. In a million ways, I know exactly what she's feeling, but I have no fucking idea what she needs. I should know what to do and how to help.

All I know is I have to see her.

Her house is full of people when I get there. There are so many bodies milling around. I just want to start tossing them aside like ragdolls until I find Peri. I shift sideways through a crowd between the kitchen and living room, and head for the hallway. I know in my gut she's either in her mom's room or her own.

I check her room first. It's empty, but my eyes linger on a discarded pile of clothes on her floor and half a dozen pairs of shoes all mixed up next to them. That part I remember—changing from one set of clothes to the next, kicking off shoes, and doing it all on autopilot.

Before I pull the door closed, I see the collection of pears pinned to a corkboard. Little pears cut out of cardboard, cans, whatever was closest when I felt like making her another one. The quilted pear my mom made is on the dresser. And the tissue-paper-covered scrap from the pear-shaped pinata I had custom-made for her seventeenth birthday is still stuck in the edge of the mirror. I remember cutting it into a pear shape with my pocketknife for her after Keller busted the pinata open like it was yesterday.

While everybody else was scavenging the spilled contents—candy and tiny liquor bottles we'd convinced Keller's older brother to buy for us—I sat at a picnic table and made sure she had a keepsake from the friends-only party I'd organized. I handed her that rainbow-ruffled pear and she smiled like I'd really given her something.

And two hours later we got arrested for spray painting on the mural at Crawford's, and our parents wouldn't let us see each other for a month. I laugh as I finish closing the door.

"Don't laugh at my mess." I take a deep breath before I turn to face her. The moment our eyes meet, she breaks, her shoulders trembling as tears rush from her eyes. "It's too soon, Bryce. I wasn't done loving her yet. It's too soon, and it's not fair."

"I know." I wrap her in my arms as her knees start to fold, and I hold her upright, not moving from the spot. "I know, Pear. I promise, I know."

"I can't breathe in there." Her eyes cut toward the living room.

I steer her into her bedroom, sit on the bed, and hold her while she screams into my chest. There are no right words, no magic to make it better, and this is the hardest thing I've ever done. I'm helpless. All I can do is be here.

A woman opens the door, talking before she even has a foot inside the room. "Peri, honey, you need to eat someth—"

"No!" I cut her off before her face registers because it doesn't matter who she is. It's rude of me, and I don't care. She backs out quickly.

Okay, so that's one thing I can do. They might mean well, but I know well right now.

"Thank you," Peri says between sobs.

"You don't have to thank me. I'll keep everyone away until you're ready. We can stay right here. There are plenty of people out there to handle things. Today, all you have to do is breathe, just be."

I scoot us up to sit against the headboard, and she holds on to me the whole time. She stops shaking, and I play with her hair while we laugh at her hiccups. There are hard days ahead for her, but if I can make this one easier, I'll take on the world.

My arm falls asleep, but it's because she's sleeping on it, so I'm not about to move an inch. The first real cold front is blowing in, and the trees outside her window look like they're dancing. There's a steady hum of voices through the wall, and the front door has opened and closed so many times, I can hear her dad in my head, yelling, "In or out! I don't own the electric company."

Every now and then, food smells waft down the hall and creep in under her door. My stomach's rumbling, but I won't move her, not even to eat. I haven't eaten at all today, though. I'm hungry and that feels selfish when she can't bring herself to eat anything.

Thinking about the emotions that might overtake her when she leaves this room again guts me. I remember walking through my parents' house for the first time after my mom died. My dad had been gone for five years, and I still wasn't used to him not being there. But that emptiness after Mom was gone, too . . . three years later, it still hits me sometimes.

At least I had Lisa and her family to lean on. Peri is an only child. She's got a network of aunts and uncles and cousins that stretches like a spider web all over the state, and some are local, but she's not really close to any of them. She's the youngest by far, a whole generation apart. It makes a difference, even with family.

I smile at us in the mirror. She's drooling on my sleeve, and she'd die if she knew, but I'm so damn glad she feels safe enough to fall asleep on me. Maybe she's just too worn out to fight it, but it feels good to think it could mean something more.

She rouses and stretches in my arms. When she sits up, she looks lost, like she's not sure where she is or what's happening for a moment, but the scope of what's happened weighs her expression down within seconds.

"Do you want me to go out there and get you something to eat?" I ask.

"No. I want to get out of this house. I know I have to face it, but right now, I want out. I want to not talk about it yet, not think about what comes next. I want to wash my face and go sit in a restaurant and eat a meal like the world will stop spinning for the rest of the day, and I can catch up tomorrow."

"I'll take you out of here to go do anything you want. We can go eat. We can do something crazy. I don't care. You name it and I'll make it happen."

"The bank's still open."

"I forgot my wig."

We both laugh, and I'm more than ready to steal her away, to help her deny grief for a few more hours. It'll keep.

Sandy Lindsey stops us on our way to the front door. "Y'all aren't leaving, are you?"

"Yes, Sandy, we are," Peri responds with more kindness and patience than I expect. She doesn't kick her out again or speak sharply. She's soft and sincere. "She left this world knowing I would take care of everything that needed to be done. And I will. But there are no urgent decisions left. She's gone, and right now, I need to fill my lungs with air that isn't shot through with absolute fucking sorrow. I don't know, nor do I care if you understand that, but I'm leaving for a little while. I'll be back when I get back."

"Well, sweetheart, you can't just do that."

"The hell she can't."

Peri puts her hand on my shoulder to let me know she's got this. "I can and I am. Everyone needs to be gone by ten."

"Will you be back before then?"

"This is my house. Literally. I own it now. And I won't be answering to anybody about when I come and go from it."

"There's a schedule. People have signed up, Peri. I can't just tell them now that they can't come at their allotted time because it's earlier than you prefer."

"Being that you're the one who allotted them the time to begin with, I think you can, and you better. I want this house quiet and empty between the hours of ten and ten. Adjust the schedule however you need to, or I'll do away with it altogether."

We leave Sandy with her mouth agape. Few others even notice. They're eating and mingling, probably sharing great stories about Marie Abshire, which is exactly the way she would've wanted it. But I'm taking her daughter as far away from it as she wants to go.

12

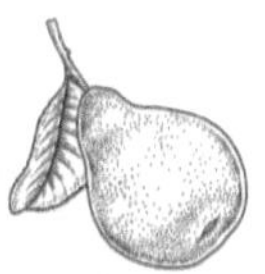

Peri

I watch the lunchtime happenings of downtown Copper through Bryce's windshield.

"What are you hungry for?" he asks.

"I don't really want to go to a restaurant. Nothing sounds good."

He angles into a parking spot in front of Donuts & More. "Nobody ever had to be hungry to eat a donut. Any requests?"

"Just get donut holes. They're easier to eat on the road."

"You're not driving, but okay." He laughs. "Do you want regular coffee or a vanilla latte?"

"Plain. Black."

"Don't go anywhere."

I smile. "No promises." He walks into the donut shop, and I flip down the visor to look at myself in the mirror. The swollen eyes and the dark circles beneath them are probably to be expected right now. When they fade, the deeper changes won't show on my face, but I'm someone different now. Parentless.

Some things that seem like they should've changed the moment she took her last breath didn't change at all. Nearly thirty and I still feeling like I'm masquerading as an adult. I have insurance paperwork to fill out, funeral arrangements to finalize, an estate to settle . . . and I'm not sure who decided I was grown enough to do any of those things. But I'm the only one who can. *Buck up, buttercup.* I push the visor back into place and put on sunglasses.

Bryce opens his door and hands me two large coffees. I fit them into his cup holders while he climbs back into the truck with three bags, two orders of donut holes, and two of my favorites, chocolate croissants, in the third bag. "I'm going to get sugar and crumbs all over your truck."

"I know how to work the vacuum at the car wash. Eat."

The first sip of the bitter coffee burns my tongue, and I take another right away. The too-hot feeling is welcome, not only for the pain that lets me know I'm not numb, but also because it's chilly out. "I didn't expect it to be this cold outside."

"There's a hoodie behind the seat if you want it."

I haven't worn one of his hoodies since I was eighteen, but I'm more than happy to turn to the backseat and grab the one he's offering. Holding it up before I pull it over my head to see what I'm about to wear, I roll my eyes at the performative patriotic image. "Really? You're one of those guys now?"

"It's from a shop owned by disabled vets, so if that's what you mean, then yes, I'm one of those guys now."

"I hope you looked into that claim. You know people say shit like that just to get your money, right?"

"They're legit."

"If you say so." The fleece lining is cozy the moment I slide my arms into it. Wearing an American flag on my chest definitely won't go down in history as the worst thing that happened in my world today. I shove two donut holes into my mouth like they're popcorn and wash them down with more of the strong coffee. There is no burn on my tongue, no chill on my arms, no physical discomfort at all. "Thank you."

"What did I tell you about thanking me?" He winks.

"That I should do it with your dick in my mouth?"

He chokes on his coffee. "Pretty sure I never said it exactly like that."

"What can I say? I've grown crude in my old age."

"As opposed to the ladylike, refined young woman you once were."

"I've heard a lot over the past month about the young woman I once was, but they all left out the words ladylike and refined."

"Well, they didn't know you like I did."

"Nobody did." Our eyes meet, and it's a snapshot moment. It's a perfect fall day, I'm warm and caffeinated, and there's literally sugar melting in my mouth. If I could freeze time . . .

He turns off Main Street, but not in a direction that would take us anywhere near a town with a five-figure population. There's nothing this way but back roads and one-stoplight towns for 60 miles. I used to know these roads. They still feel familiar, but I don't remember any of the forks or the curves, the fields or the fences that go on forever.

The wildflowers are all gone already, nothing to see for miles but small churches, smaller houses, cows, and goats. We go around a curve and there's a herd of bison grazing in the sun just past the sign for a new subdivision that's still being built. We top a hill and there are zebras. Zebras! I sit straight up. They've always been my favorite, but I've never seen one outside a zoo. Bryce eases onto the shoulder and parks.

"Is this one of those drive-through safari places?"

"Yeah, we're on the back side of it. These zebras are usually hanging out over here in the mornings. I didn't want to tell you where we were going in case they weren't here today. You want to get out and get a closer look?"

"Can we pet them?"

"No. There's a double fence. You can't get that close to them."

"Um, hello. You've seen me climb a fence."

"I'm not going to see you climb these."

"Fine." I pull on the handle to open my door and hop down onto the gravel.

He's right. Even if I managed to get over the barbed wire on the first fence, there's a much higher wild game fence beyond it, separating us from the zebras. I've been closer to them in zoos, but I've never seen this many. "How'd they get all these zebras?"

"I don't know. I've never asked."

"Do you know the owner?"

"Yeah, he's the developer of that new subdivision we just passed. I've done some work for him."

"For the record, I could climb that high fence easily."

"It's not the high one you should be worried about."

"Yeah, I know. But I want to know how they got here. Is it a zebra rescue or did he trap them and steal them from their home? Do they need to be rescued from him?"

"I'll see what I can find out."

He steps behind me and wraps his arms around my waist, and we stand on the side of the road and watch these displaced zebras, grazing in the shade, occasionally casting wary glances our way. They're so beautiful but they're making me sad. I know Bryce brought me here to make me smile, and that's really sweet, but they shouldn't be fenced in.

"They sound like Crash when he's barking in his sleep," he says.

They do make the weirdest sounds. "When I was a little girl, I thought they were mythical, like unicorns. The first time I saw one was in the Fort Worth Zoo . . ." I trail off, laughing because I remember he already knows this about me.

"You didn't want to leave them, not even when your mom told you there were real elephants and hippos and tigers to see. Your dad tried to lure you away by saying Simba was there, but you wouldn't leave until he promised you ice cream."

"And I cried myself to sleep that night because we forgot to take a picture of me with the zebras, so he drove two hours to take me back the next weekend. He took a dozen pictures of me posing in front of them. To this day, Zebras and ice cream are still two of my favorite things."

He kisses the top of my head, and I'm reminded how much taller than me he is. I never felt smaller than him unless I saw a picture of us. When we were together, I felt every bit his equal in strength and size. I knew I was every bit as bold, every bit as much of a thrill seeker.

So much of the reckless shit we did, we were just trying to outdo each other. Impress each other. A couple bored kids with wild streaks too big for our own good.

And today, he buys me donuts and brings me to see roadside zebras. I pull my phone from the front pocket of his hoodie, and he immediately reaches for it. "I'll take your picture."

"Our picture."

I leave my sunglasses on, and he gets the angle all wrong, but it's not terrible. Nothing to cry myself to sleep over.

13

Bryce

THIS GIRL WHO USED to be larger than life feels so small in my arms right now. She doesn't know it yet and wouldn't believe me if I told her, but she'll feel big and bold again. This is temporary.

"You remember the dairy farm that used to be out here? We'd pass it on the way to the river?"

"The one with the tiny ice cream shop connected to their offices? First, you get me donuts and take me to see zebras, and now you're offering me ice cream? This is like nine-year-old Peri's dream date."

"It's a winery now."

"Oh, my bad. It's twenty-nine-year-old Peri's dream date. Yes, please."

She's trying so hard to compartmentalize, keep death at home where it happened and not let it follow her out in the world. It'll work for today. I'm here to orchestrate the diversions, but when she has to face it, I'll still be here.

We grab a picnic table under an oak tree at the winery. I watch as she twirls her glass and lets the wine slosh up the sides. She stares at it as if something miraculous is happening in the movement.

"When did you know you were going to be okay with neither one of your parents in the world?" she asks.

"I don't know. I just woke up one day and stopped asking why."

"Acceptance."

"It comes."

"Okay." She tilts her glass from side-to-side, dipping and lifting like she's drawing the infinity sign. "I don't remember how it went after my dad died, how long anything took."

"Might've been different because you still had your mom."

"Yeah."

I don't think she's taken a single sip yet, but if making waves in her glass helps soothe her, I don't care if she drinks it at all. "Still seems wild our dads died together in that wreck," she says. "I think about it a lot."

"Friends till the end," I say. "Even when they didn't want their kids anywhere near each other anymore."

"And then our moms both die of cancer three years apart. That's a lot of shared tragedy."

"We've shared more than tragedy, Pear."

"I know. I'm sorry. You don't need me to reopen all your wounds."

"It's not like that. It helps to talk about it sometimes."

"Despite everything, you made me a better person, Bryce. I can't imagine what my life would've looked like if I'd never known you."

"You'd have gone to your first-choice college."

"Which ended up not mattering at all. I have a great job, and neighbors who don't even know about the time I got kicked out of Pizza Palace for flashing my boyfriend on stage on karaoke night."

"We'd have gotten kicked out for our improvised lyrics, whether you showed your tits or not."

"Improvised." She laughs. "We spent hours coming up with that shit."

"I always thought it was time well spent."

"Because it resulted in you seeing my boobs in public."

"Totally worth all the places we got kicked out of."

"It's a wonder we never got arrested." She finally takes a sip of her wine. "For that, I mean."

"See, there's another thing that wouldn't have happened without me. You would've never been arrested."

"Oh, I'd have been arrested, but probably for a lot worse than a three-foot-high neon green dick."

"That was art."

"Me, the misunderstood artist. And they just kept power-washing away my legacy."

"Speaking of legacies." I pull my phone out of my pocket and bring up the picture Keller sent me last night.

"Aw, is that Catie's new baby?"

"That's her. Isabella Peri."

"Wait, what? She named her baby after me?"

"According to Keller, she always said you were the strongest, bravest girl she ever knew, and if she had a daughter, she was going to name her after you. He says they're going to call her Bella, but I might have to call her Peri."

"Don't you dare curse that perfect little girl like that."

"It's already her name. And it's far from a curse." I lift my glass, and she does the same. "Cheers to the next generation."

"May they be better than us," she says.

"They won't be. But they'll probably turn out all right, too."

We finish our wine, and she has a second glass while I nurse a bottle of water. "You want to go swimming?"

"Where?"

"I know a great pool back in Copper. Behind a big house on Magnolia Lane."

She tosses her head back and laughs. "No, thanks. I've already been arrested for trespassing in that pool."

"It's not the mayor's house anymore. It's a bed and breakfast, and I know for a fact it's currently being remodeled, so there are no guests staying there."

"Like I said, already tried it. Come up with something original for once, why don't you?"

"Give me time. I'll get us arrested for something good."

"If I'm getting arrested at this point in my life, it better be something spectacular."

"Any chance I could get you to eat some real food?"

"I'll try."

I hold her hand on the walk back to my truck. I reached out of instinct, and she laced her fingers with mine.

"You know what would be spectacular and totally worth getting arrested for?" she asks. "Setting those zebras free."

"How about we aim for a spectacular misdemeanor, not a felony."

"Chicken."

14

Peri

WHEN THE WAITER COMES over, I look at the menu one last time and order the first thing I see: a pulled pork sandwich. I'm pretty sure everything would taste the same to me right now, so it doesn't matter. I don't feel hungry, but I don't want people to start hovering around me, worrying that I'm not eating.

"Have you been on leave from work this whole time?" Bryce asks while we wait for our food.

"No, I can work remote. I put in about thirty hours the first few weeks I was here, and then started tapering off as she got worse. I texted my boss this morning, so I'm officially on leave now. But I may work some just to keep my mind occupied. Who knows?"

"Don't push yourself if you don't have to." He takes away the sugar packet I've been kneading. "You're listening to me, right?"

"Right. Don't push myself." I take a fresh packet from the container at the edge of the table.

I manage to eat about half my sandwich, which is more than I expected. He's been done with his sandwich and his fries for a while now, so I shove my plate across the table to him. "You can finish this if you want. I'm done."

"You could take it home."

"I won't eat it. Besides, have you seen the amount of food people have crammed into my fridge and freezer? I'm one person and they've brought enough to feed a whole family for three months. I will never eat all that stuff. Do you think Keller and Catie might want some of it?"

"That's a good idea. It'd take some of the load off her mom and Keller."

"Do you mind taking it to them?"

"No, of course not. They'd love to see you, though. When you're feeling up to it."

"I'll make a point to see them before I leave."

He gets quiet after I mention leaving. It's not just that he doesn't say anything; his whole demeanor is quiet.

"I probably have enough cakes and cookies to keep their boys in desserts until Christmas."

"Never met a kid who didn't want dessert."

"Should I go back? Is it wrong to stay gone this long?"

"No. You said it best yourself. It's your house, and you can come and go as you please. It's none of anybody else's business."

"I know, but . . . I keep thinking my mom would say I should be there."

"I'll take you back whenever you want. If you want company, I'll stay."

"Yeah, it'd be easier if you were there."

"Come on. Let's go do the meet and grief."

My laughter builds as I realize what he's said. It takes a few seconds for me to get it, but I'm so glad he's not censoring himself around me. No matter what, I know I can count on him to be real.

I foolishly hope there will be no cars there when we turn onto Hollyhock, the street that claimed skin from my knees and elbows when I skated over a stick or lost control of my bike, and years later, stole tears from my eyes when I put it in the rearview mirror, and swore I was never coming back.

The driveway is full, and there are still cars and trucks parked in front of the neighbors' houses on both sides of the street.

"More is better," he says, reading my expression. "When there are only a few, you have to talk to them longer. This way, they can talk to each other, and you can move between them without getting stuck in a conversation you don't want to have with people you don't want to look at."

"Thanks. I needed some perspective."

"Mine might not always be the politest, but it'll be honest."

"I appreciate that about you more than you know."

There are partially-eaten casseroles and crackers and cheese and chips and trays of raw veggies and dips and deli meat and loaves of bread and cookies and muffins and pies everywhere. Every square inch of table and counter space is covered with plates and dishes. It makes my body thrum with anxiety. If I had to clean this all up, I'd drop to my knees and cry. So much of this food is going to be wasted, and that's such a shame.

Be gracious. It's what she would want.

I never knew how badly my neck and jaw could ache from forcing a smile and gently nodding at the same comments over and over—and from holding back responses that would only make everyone uncomfortable. My mom held her tongue her entire life when there was so much she wanted to say. Surely, I can do it for a few days.

After a while, the faces and voices become nondescript. They comment, I smile. They ask, I answer.

"She was always so proud of you."

I smile.

"Did she have her arrangements made before she passed?"

I nod and say, "For the most part. I'm meeting with the funeral home tomorrow to finalize everything."

"People have been asking about the services. No one could find you, so I called over to Lowenstein's and they said the chapel is available Wednesday and Friday, but it's already booked for Thursday."

I take a deep breath. "I'm sitting down with them in the morning. It will probably be Wednesday."

"I started a memorial page on Facebook. If you could share the details there for the date and time of her services, I'm sure people would appreciate it."

My eye twitches. "I'm sorry, you did what?"

Bryce's hands cup my shoulders as he steps closer from behind. "The funeral home will update it on their website," he says. "You can, of course, feel free to share whatever information they provide on the page you created. Peri's going to have her hands full for the next few days. I'm sure you understand."

The front door opens, and Bryce's sister, Lisa walks in. It's just her, and she's not carrying any cream-of-nausea soup casserole. She has a plain brown paper bag in her hand, and I've never been happier to see her. We move toward each other.

She wraps me in a tight hug and whispers, "Whatever you do, don't make eye contact with any of them. That's how they steal your soul."

"It's good to see you," I say.

"You don't have to lie to me. Nothing is good right now. I know. I remember." She holds the bag out. "I know she didn't allow alcohol in her house, but it's your house now, so I figured you could decide."

"I'll allow it." I smile and slide the bottle out of the bag enough to see it's whiskey. "Good call."

"Like I said, I remember." She waves at her brother, and then she pulls me through the crowd to the sliding glass door and into the backyard. "Breathe."

"I'm okay. Bryce got me out of here before lunch. We've only been back about an hour, I think." We lean against the back of the house, out of view of the inquisitive mourners. I pull the stopper from the bottle and take a swig.

"Aw, look at my little brother," she says, "knowing what to do in a crisis like he's all grown up."

I laugh and pass the bottle to her. He hated the way she acted like his second mother when we were growing up, but she's fourteen years older than us. I used to think she was born old. She doesn't seem so old now, though. "Speaking of being all grown up, I saw pictures of the kids at Bryce's."

"Oh, they just think they're grown. Eighteen and twenty. Babies."

"I remember."

She laughs. "You thought you were grown long before eighteen."

"And now, I wake up every day wondering when it's going to happen."

"That never goes away." She takes another swallow, and hands the whiskey back to me. "That's it for me."

Lisa was never a big drinker. And I'm not one tonight, so I hit the bottle once more and put the stopper back in the neck. "Thanks."

"You staying in town for a while?"

"I'll probably leave sometime next week, and handle what needs to be done to sell the house and settle the rest of her estate by phone and email."

"I sure wish you'd stick around a little longer."

"Nothing's definite right now. But if you're worried about Bryce, he'll be fine. He really is all grown up, Lisa."

"If you'd asked me a month ago, I'd have said he was over you. But the day he found out you were back I knew he wasn't."

"He's moved on. There have been other women in his life."

"Not for long. And I don't see a ring on your finger."

"That is not on my bucket list."

"Don't go running off again without saying goodbye."

"I won't. Any chance I could use your discount to buy a new curling iron while I'm here?"

"I've got an extra one at the salon that I never use. I won it, but I already have one just like it. It's a good one, just taking up space in a drawer at my station. Swing by and grab it anytime." She stares at me for a moment, and then she hugs me again. "I know hiding feels best, but you have to go back in there."

"Are you sure?"

"You can take breaks, but you've got to see it through. It'll be over soon, I promise."

"Not soon enough."

She pulls me back inside the same way she dragged me out. I detour to my room to hide the whiskey. The thought that I could close and lock my door and not come out until everyone has left is so appealing, but I can't leave Bryce out there alone.

The crowd is starting to thin out. Sandy Lindsey is supervising the kitchen clean up. More power to her.

I sneak out to the backyard alone. Bryce follows a few minutes later. "You okay?"

"Yeah, just needed to breathe again."

"Can I stay with you tonight?"

"What about Crash?"

"Lisa has a key. She is going by to let him out and give him some food and water on her way home."

I hear his sister's words again and feel her concern when I look at him. It's a cloudy night, no bright moon to light up his eyes, but they shine in the darkness, anyway. If I tell him no, I'm sending him home to worry about me. If I say yes, I don't have to be alone and he doesn't have to worry. When I looked around at all the people in my house, all I wanted was to be alone. But when I look at him, being alone is the last thing I want. "Yeah, if it doesn't interrupt your life too much, of course you can stay."

"Interrupt my life, Peri. It'll be fine."

After the last person leaves, I expect to feel lighter, for the house to feel expansive and calming, but the weight of her absence is suddenly so heavy, as if all the talking, eating people had been holding it up, and now it's caving in on me.

"A hot shower might feel good," he says.

"I'm not sure I have the energy."

"I'll help."

"I definitely don't have the energy for that."

He smiles. "That's not what I meant. Come on."

Taking a shower doesn't seem important, but not taking one seems pathetic. "Okay."

There is nothing seductive in the way he undresses us. He checks the temperature of the shower with his hand before he leads me into it. It does feel good. I tilt my head back to soak my hair, and I feel like I could stand here for hours, but Bryce turns me and starts to massage shampoo from my scalp to the ends of my hair. I let him turn me again when it's time to rinse. He reaches for the conditioner without me having to tell him.

I face the falling water while he runs a loofah over my back, and I honestly can't tell if I'm crying or if it's just the spray from the shower rolling down my cheeks. I don't know if I'm standing or he's holding me up. I'm not sure if any of this is even real, if today happened at all.

When he shuts off the water, I wring out my hair. He wraps a towel around his waist, passes me one for my hair and waits while I wrap it up before he hands me one to dry my body. These little things we do in sync. Muscle memory from all the nights we spent together after lying to our parents about where we'd be and with whom, mostly sneaking off to his aunt's lake house. His cousin was always a reliable source of when it would be available, and we never missed an opportunity.

Lisa's right. We were babies. But at least we weren't getting into any trouble when we were alone at the lake.

Running a comb through my wet hair, I say, "Go forage in the fridge. I know you're probably hungry again."

"I could eat."

"Go do that. I'm just going to dry my hair a little."

I point the hair dryer at my head, making no effort to style it or tame it. All I want is for it be somewhat dry before I crawl into bed. After I comb out the resulting tangles in my mostly dry hair, I go to the living room and find Bryce on the couch with a plate of spaghetti. He offers me a spiraled forkful when I sit next to him, but I shake my head. I take a bite from one of the cookies he's set on the coffee table, but it doesn't taste like anything.

Of all the places we took risky chances, we were never brave enough to push our luck in this house. I fold the covers back and slide into bed, holding them open for him. "First time for everything."

"I was just thinking that. Your dad would've killed me with his bare hands if he'd ever caught me in your bed. Your mama might've come close."

"She might've succeeded, actually. It took a lot to piss her off, but once she got there, she was pretty fierce."

"You don't have to tell me."

All the ill-advised bullshit I did growing up felt like the only way to survive sometimes. There was always so much antsy need for more, for constant excitement and boundary pushing, but I was as afraid of getting caught as anyone. I just didn't let it stop me.

My fears are all different now, but I still can't resist doing scary things, like letting him stay with me all night long. The thought of waking up in his arms terrifies me, but all I can do is settle against him and let it happen.

15

Bryce

I WAKE TO HER body convulsing, and attempted cries being strangled before she can release them. She's having a bad dream, and she's trying to scream, but can't. She always used to do this when she was stressed. Holding her close to me, I whisper, "You're okay, Pear. I'm right here. It's just a dream."

Her eyes flutter open, and I tighten my hold on her. As soon as she realizes she's caught in my arms, the thrashing begins. She's still terrified, not fully awake. I don't want to make her panic, but I also don't want to be on the receiving end of it with her limbs free. It takes a few moments for her to realize what's happening.

She looks around the room wide-eyed, but clearly unsure of where she's at. And then it hits her all at once, and the tears burst. She buries her face in my chest, and I loosen my grip, but keep my arms around her and let her cry.

When her tears are replaced by dry sobs, I brush her damp hair away from her face, and make her look at me. "It's gonna be okay. I promise." This is exactly why I wanted to stay. I couldn't stand the possibility that this might happen and she'd be all alone. Fuck,

I can't stand the thought of leaving her at all until I know she's on the other side of this pain and the grief, and I already know that's going to take more time than she's willing to give.

She's going to leave before I'm ready, before she's ready, but I can't worry about that because she's here now, and this is exactly where she should be. With me. "I'm here, Pear. I've got you."

Her mouth closes on mine and her kiss is so desperate it breaks my heart, but I need her to need me like this. A light sheen of sweat coats her body, and my hands glide over her skin as I push her tank top up. She grabs for it and pulls it over her head, tossing it aside. The salt from her sweat turns sweet on my tongue as I draw her nipple into my mouth and begin to suck. My dick throbs when she moans. Her surrender turns me inside out like it always has. I know what she wants, what I need, who we are.

I release her nipple and drag her under me, pinning her wrists to the pillow above her head while my other hand removes her thin shorts. She rocks her hips to help me take them off. My hand cups her soft pussy, and the heat filling my palm feels so good. I close my eyes for a moment and let the sensation catch up to the memories before I begin to massage it, causing her juices to escape and run across my fingers, making them slippery. I slide one, then two inside her.

Alternating between her nipples, I suck and nibble until she pulls her shoulder to retreat, welcoming me back to the other side and taking it for a little longer on each return. She starts to writhe beneath me when I graze her clit with my thumb and circle a few times before denying her more.

"Same word?"

She nods with her eyes half-closed, and I know she doesn't want to leave the state of agitation I've put her in unless it's to go further. "Whose pussy am I playing with?"

"Yours." Her voice is breathy and soft.

"It's mine? Just mine?"

No response. I know I shouldn't push this, but I can't help myself. I need to hear her say it, whether it's true anymore or not.

"Do you want to share it with anybody else?"

"Only if you tell me to."

Oh, fuck. That's a new response. And I don't hate it.

"Did you feel your nipples get harder when you said that? I'm pretty sure you could cut glass with them right now." I tease my tongue around one of the stiff peaks.

She bucks her hips. "Pretty sure you could drive nails with this hard dick."

"The only thing my dick wants to drive is you into this mattress."

"Do it then."

"Not until you scream for me. We're all alone. And I want to hear you scream."

I pull my fingers from her pussy and bring them to her lips. She lolls her tongue between them, and then she sucks the tips into her mouth before she pulls off, leaving a glistening string between her bottom lip and my fingers. I shove them into her parted mouth, and she sucks them fully, licking her arousal off my skin.

The desire to taste it with her wins out over the need to watch her do it alone. I retract my fingers a few inches and kiss her, our tongues flicking around my knuckles to touch.

"You taste so good. Your sweet little cunt is spilling everywhere, and I haven't even made you come yet." I slide my fingers back into her pussy. "Squeeze those tight silky walls, show me how it's going to feel when you're milking my cock. Yeah, that's it, such an obedient little slut, my private whore. I always loved it when my good girl was bad for me."

"We were bad for each other, remember?"

"But we were so good at being bad together. And it seems like that dirty girl I knew grew into an even dirtier woman."

"That dirty talking boy I knew has upped his game, too."

I lift up to look into her eyes. "Let's play."

"I'm waiting."

I slide my fingers up to spread her arousal over her clit. It's swollen and sensitive enough to make her gasp when I knead it between my fingers. I press hard with the pad of my thumb to gauge her reaction. "Do you want me to back off, be gentler and let it build?"

"You can do whatever you want, however you want."

"So, this is okay?" I smash my thumb into her clit and she arches her back. "Don't run away from me." I press hard circles and she sucks in a sharp breath, but her body starts to quiver and I know her offer wasn't lip service; she wants it rough. All of it.

Keeping up my direct assault on her clit, I squeeze her wrists tighter and go back to sucking her nipple, staying on one as I suck harder, press harder and faster with my thumb, let my teeth help ratchet up the pain until she's so close to screaming I can feel the strain vibrating in her chest. *Do it. Scream for me.*

Her spine jolts and her thighs trap my hand between her legs as the sound finally leaves her mouth. It's broken and choppy and the most beautiful scream I've ever heard. She doesn't say my name, and I never needed her to. All I needed was for her to let out everything she's ever held back. I wanted to give her the release that can't form words, can't make sense, can't ask or beg or plead or acknowledge in any possible way other than that shrieking expulsion of pain and anger and bliss all swirled together and leaving her body like a demon being exorcised.

She quakes with an aftershock, and I relax my hand as her legs soften to release it. I let go of her wrists, and she opens and closes her fingers a few times, but leaves her arms up with her hands now resting above her head as she continues to come down from her orgasm.

"You weren't supposed to give me a break," she says.

She always loved it when I started to fuck her as soon as her orgasm started to wane, when her pussy was still clenched and nearly too tight for my dick to enter, but she needed a break this time. "No break next time."

"Why this time? Because I'm so fragile?"

"Oh, I have no intention of treating you like you're fragile. Roll over."

She flips onto her stomach and starfishes to bait me. To be a brat. But I'm not in the mood to argue, so I simply knee her legs farther apart and thrust my cock into her slick pussy without lifting her hips up or asking if this is okay. She'll tell me if it's not.

Even with the break to recover, I can feel her stretching as my cock pushes deeper, her walls pulling me in. That magnetic pull. *Fuck, yes.*

Her forearms sink into the mattress when she pulls them close to her side, plants them, and attempts to rise up. I shove her back down, but she does it again, so I gather her hair in my hand and pull. From her chest up, she's lifted off the mattress, but her lower body is still splayed flat against it while I pump into her, keeping tension in the ponytail I've created in my fist. I groan at the sight of her neck craned back and her pretty ass shaking every time I slam into her.

I reach around to squeeze her tit and pinch the nipple I've already punished with my mouth. She whimpers and her pussy spasms.

My body responds like she's flipped a switch, muscles contracting, and breathing accelerating until I'm shooting my load inside her. We both collapse, and I can feel my hot come leaking back out around my spent cock. If she knew how much smug satisfaction that feeling provides me, she'd probably kick me out. The possessive need to claim her, to own her, is as strong as it ever was in this moment. And I don't have this moment with anyone else.

16

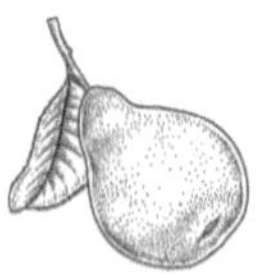

Peri

I STEP BACK INTO my room quietly, but Bryce is sitting up in my bed, looking at his phone. "How'd you get out of this bed without waking me up?"

"You sleep like the dead." I inhale sharply as if it might take back the comment. Sometimes, the irreverent shit that comes out of my mouth surprises me as much as it does anyone, but Bryce isn't fazed.

"Speaking of, do you want me to go to the funeral home with you this morning?"

"No. I want you to go to your shop and carry on with your life without feeling like you need to babysit me." I toss his pants at him. "But thank you for staying last night. I'm glad you were here. And not just for the sex." I smile, hoping to dispel the pollution of words like *dead* and *funeral*.

"I know. I'm glad I was here, too."

He starts to get dressed, and I rummage through my suitcase. "I didn't bring clothes for the big event or the planning of it. I think in some twisted way, I thought if I didn't pack funeral clothes, maybe she wouldn't die. How fucked up is that?" So much for not using the poison words.

"Everybody bargains. It's not supposed to make sense. Nobody at Lowenstein's is going to care what you're wearing. And I guarantee with one text you could find a shopping partner more than willing to help you pick out something for the funeral."

"I don't like to shop with other people." I settle on a pair of dark jeans and a sweater, but I can't decide what shoes to wear. "She opened her eyes and talked to me."

"What?"

"A few hours before she died." I grab socks because I'm going with boots. "I'm sorry. I just needed to say it out loud to convince myself it was real."

"You can say whatever you want to me. You know that. But of course, it was real."

"She looked right at me and talked for a few minutes straight, mostly about the people who were waiting for her. They were apparently in the room with us, but she didn't name anyone, just kept saying *they* are here and *they* say I have to go soon. She didn't seem afraid. She didn't even seem sick. But then she closed her eyes and went back to sleep. I was awake when she died, but that was hours later. I know it sometimes happens, a death rally or whatever, but I couldn't ask her anything before it was over. I couldn't speak. All I could do was stare at her."

"You did everything you needed to, Pear. You were there, and that's all she needed from you."

I sigh. "And now I have to do what comes next."

"Say the word, and I can clear my day."

"You hate shopping."

"I could wait in the truck for that part."

"Quit trying to use me to get out of work."

"My phone will be on."

"Thanks, but I've got this." I open my closet and lift the hanger with the clothes she wanted to be buried in. She picked them out months ago and hung them in here so I wouldn't have to go into her room so soon after she died. No shoes because she thought it was frivolous to be buried in them when somebody else could use them. All her shoes and the rest of her clothes are going to the church thrift shop, but not today.

I pull open a dresser drawer and get the small box that contains the costume jewelry she picked out. "I wanted to bury her in her wedding ring, her diamond studs, and the sapphire pendant Daddy gave her for their twenty-fifth anniversary, but she made me promise to keep those things, and bury her in this cheap stuff." My hand shakes as I hold up the box. Bryce takes it and the hanger from me.

He kisses my forehead and lets his lips stay there for a moment before he pulls away. We walk out together. I know he waited for me so we could leave at the same time because he's still afraid to leave me alone in the house, but I don't mind. That's Bryce.

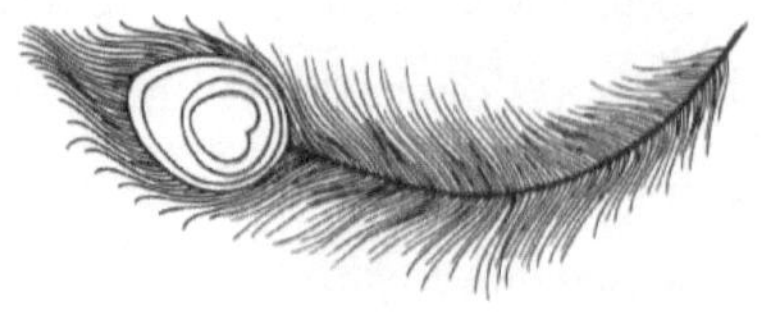

The funeral director has all the details for the service already. All I really need to do is approve the obituary for their website and nail down the date and time, decide if I want any add-ons or changes. And give them the box and the clothes. Leaving those things with them is harder than I thought it would be.

When I pull out of the parking lot, I head straight for downtown Copper. There are new boutiques on Main Street. I'm sure each one is as overpriced as the next, and I'll probably see people I know, but I don't care. I need some part of this to be easy, and doing my shopping close to home sounds easier than driving somewhere else to avoid people or price tags.

Katie with a K pokes her head out from behind a rack in the second store. She makes a beeline for me with outstretched arms. "Peri, I am so sorry."

I accept the hug. "Thanks, Katie. The services are Wednesday morning at ten. I'll call you soon about listing the house."

"Take your time with that. Don't make any quick decisions, okay?"

"I almost drove out of town to shop because I was afraid I'd run into somebody I knew, but I'm glad you're here. Can you spread the word about the funeral, please? It's already up on the funeral home's website, but I know there are probably people asking around about it."

"I'll send a group text, and the whole town will know by the end of the day."

"Some things never change."

"Speaking of things not changing, you and Bryce still look good together."

"Me and Bryce being together was a long time ago." I slide hangers along a rack and consider dresses. "He was just being a friend when you saw us in Jolene's, trying to take my mind off things. That's all."

"If you say so."

"I just did." A bright blue dress catches my eye. "Outside of Copper, I wouldn't think twice about wearing this to a funeral, but how many eyebrows do you think it'll raise if I wear it here?"

"Since when do you worry about raising anybody's eyebrows? Who cares what they think? What would your mom have said about it?"

"She liked me in jewel tones, always said I wore too much black. Basically, if it's a shade that could be found in a peacock feather, she wanted me to wear it."

"Then tell anybody who comments that she approved it, and hers is the only opinion that you give a hot goddamn about at the moment."

"That's good, Katie. Almost sounded like you were channeling me."

"I have years' worth of memories to pull from."

I lay the blue dress over my arm and laugh while I keep looking.

"Of course, making new memories can be good, too." She winks. And that's the moment I remember that Bryce's truck was in my driveway overnight.

"Is nothing sacred in this town?"

"Girl, don't ask that like you didn't grow up here." She pulls a different blue dress from a rack on the wall and hands it to me as if she's my personal shopper. "You may not have robbed a bank, but you stole that boy's heart when he was sixteen. And I'm pretty sure you've still got it."

"And I'm absolutely sure we're not having this conversation. But I will try on this dress. Thank you."

"You're welcome. I'm here, Peri. Whatever you need."

"Can you run interference and keep Sandy Lindsey away from me at the funeral?"

"I'll try. But I have to be nice about it because I manage a few rental properties for her."

"Well, I might not be nice to her if she gets too close, so I appreciate any effort you can give."

"I'm sure Bryce isn't going to let anyone who might upset you get too close."

"He's not my bodyguard," I sing-song.

"I bet he thinks he is," she sing-songs right back, and then she shoves a purple dress at me. "Go try these on. I'm going to see if I can find anything in teal that might work."

"Tell everyone in that group text I said not to wear black."

"I'll have the whole gang peacocking, babe. Don't you worry."

If anybody can convince people to wear bright colors to a funeral, it's Katie with a K. Hell, she got me to sing dirty karaoke after all these years. And she's probably the reason half the town knows Bryce spent the night at my house last night. Sometimes you have to take the bad with the good. She's Copper to her core, but I still kind of love her.

A wrap sweater dress invades my dressing room through the side of the curtain. It's bright teal and has a huge peacock feather printed on the outer edge of the wrap. It runs from the shoulder all the way to the hem. The colors in the feather are all the brightest jewel tones with golden and coppery accents.

As I'm marveling at the odds that she has actually found this outrageous dress, a pair of peacock feather earrings come dancing into view.

"Oh. My. God. I will look like the damn queen of the peacocks."

"You were always the queen, Peri."

"Well, damn, how am I supposed to say no to it, now? I draw the line at a feathered headband, just so we're clear."

"You better hope I don't find one. Actually, I could go to the craft store and make us all feathered headbands. Or better yet, ball caps and we could all wear ponytails."

"I will list that house with another realtor, Katie."

She cackles on the other side of the curtain. "I've got to get to a showing, but I'm putting these earrings on the counter. Do not leave without them."

"What choice do I have? I mean, this dress is so plain without the earrings."

The bells on the door chime, and I know she's already gone.

I come out of the fitting room to see myself in better light, and I add a pair of knee-high black dress boots. "What do you think about this outfit for a funeral?" I ask the sales clerk on the floor. She's probably mid-fifties, and for all I know, she owns the place.

"Whose funeral?"

"My mother's."

"What would she think about it?"

"Well, it's not black and there's no denim, so I'm pretty sure she'd be thrilled."

"That's the only opinion that should matter."

"Yeah. And I guess if the whole town's going to be looking at you anyway, you may as well peacock."

"Words to live by."

"I'll take the dress, the boots, and the feather earrings on the counter."

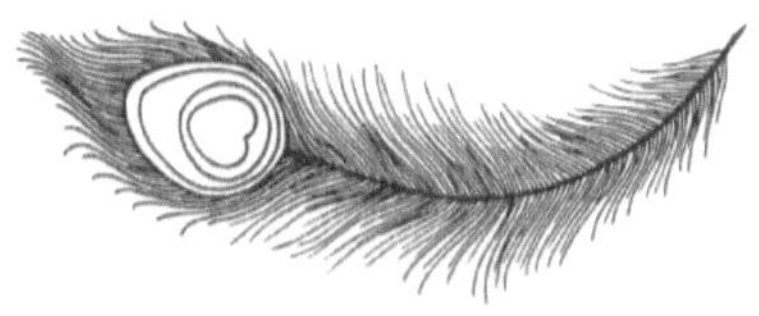

I message Catie with a C when I leave the boutique to congratulate her on the new baby. I'm not sure if she'll be awake or if the hospital lets you sleep whenever you want after you give birth. Or if they even have wi-fi. She might not see my message for days, but I feel better for sending it, anyway.

She responds immediately.

Catie: *Please come by the house anytime to meet her. You can come right now if you want. I'm so bored. Come entertain me.*

How can anyone be bored with four kids? Wait, what's she doing home already?

Peri: *Aren't you still in the hospital?*

Catie: *No, we're home. Keller is here, too. He can watch the boys while we catch up.*

Peri: *Okay, if you're sure. Send me the address.*

Catie: *Yay!*

I don't have a gift or any idea if it's really okay to go to someone's house this soon after they bring home a newborn, but Catie seems happy about it, and I need somewhere to go that isn't my mom's house, so I'm going.

The three stair-stepped little boys I've seen in pictures come running out the front door as soon as I pull up. All blonde like Keller, and full of energy like Catie.

"Are you our mom's friend?"

"I am. Hi. My name's Peri."

"I'm Easton."

"I'm Weston."

Keller steps up behind them, and I look at him in astonishment.

"What? She named the first one Easton, but she promised I could name the second one." He gives me his trademark smirky grin. "I thought it was funny. Most people don't even get it. Easton and Weston are both common names."

"Probably not for brothers, Keller."

I turn to the third little boy, the youngest. "Who are you, Northon or Southon?"

Poor kid looks totally confused. "I'm just Tyson."

"It's nice to meet you, just Tyson."

"All right, anybody who's going to the store for snacks, load up." All three boys run for their dad's truck. "Catie's feeding Bella. Just go on in."

I pause on the porch and look back to watch Keller fasten seatbelts and booster seats. That seems like a lot of responsibility for a man who named his second kid for the sake of a joke. Catie yells, "Come in here right now!"

She's on the couch with a baby attached to her boob. "Sit. Enjoy this peace and quiet with me before the terrible trio gets back."

"There are four of them if you count your maniac of a husband."

"Yeah, but he wreaks his havoc more quietly." If it had been eighty years since I'd seen her instead of eight, I'd still recognize that bubbly laugh.

"Keller is buckling car seats and you're breastfeeding . . . I feel like I've stepped into an alternate dimension."

"That's how I feel every morning when I wake up." She laughs again. "You want to hold her?"

"No, I don't hold newborns."

"They're not as fragile as they look."

"Given that middle name you saddled her with, she better not be fragile."

Catie smiles. "I can't wait until she has enough hair for a pony-tail."

"I'll buy her first ballcap."

"If you could come in clutch with bail money, too, that would be good because, you know, we've got all these mouths to feed."

"Listen, I'm still in my own ponytail bandit era. I have to save all the bail money for myself."

"Bullshit. Bryce has filled us in. You're a raging success of an artist, living your fancy life in Houston in your fancy apartment, driving your fancy car."

"You know Bryce exaggerates. I'm a graphic designer, and I'm still just me."

"No, you're not that girl who left here. I miss that girl some-times, but I'm proud of you."

"If I'm being honest, I miss that girl sometimes, too. That's probably why it's so easy to hang out with Bryce, which I probably shouldn't be doing at all."

"Are you happy?"

"Yeah. I mean, my work's not hanging in galleries in New York. Reality looks a little different from the dream, but I still paint, sell a few pieces here and there. Life's good."

"You know that's not what I meant."

"Don't go there, Catie. We were kids."

"And now you're adults. And you're both still single. And I don't think that's a coincidence."

"Apparently, you're not the only Catie in town who feels that way."

"People with other names feel that way, too."

"People should find something else to talk about."

"Okay. Okay. How long are you staying?"

"Services are Wednesday morning. I'll probably head home next week."

"That's so soon. I probably won't be able to make it Wednesday." She nods at the drowsy baby in her arms. "But you'll be in my thoughts."

"Bella is the only one who needs to be in your thoughts on Wednesday. And those ridiculously-named little boys. Why the hell'd you let Keller do that?"

She shrugs. "I can't help it. I still think he's funny. And the boys think he's hilarious."

"Your parents never found him so amusing. How's that going these days?"

"They've come around. He still turns everything into a joke, but he's grown up. We all have. Saw the video of your karaoke performance in Jolene's, by the way."

"Oh, shit. I knew there was probably video evidence of that."

We relive memories of every place Bryce and I got kicked out of for performing that song, including the county fair. It's true what they say about the brain protecting you from certain memories. But was someone ever really a friend if they can't mine the most embarrassing moments from your psyche?

Before I know it, she's got me holding baby Bella while she flips through our senior yearbook and updates me on people I haven't thought about in years. It seems I'm not the only one who doesn't share every detail of my life on social media. Catie's got some dirt on a few people I follow whose online lives do not mirror their real lives in the least.

People still trust her with all their secrets. It's those big blue eyes and that sweet smile.

And she still repeats everything she knows. She never could help herself, which is why when she points at a picture of Bryce, throwing the winning touchdown in a playoff game, and says, "Look me in the eyes and tell me you're not still in love with that boy," I look right at her and swear I'm not.

I look back at that photo of a boy who doesn't exist anymore, and the hot mess of a girl who is on her feet in the stands, out of view of the camera lens, screaming like the outcome of a football game is going to make a difference in either of their lives.

All their life-changing events are months away from that night, but they don't have a clue.

17

Bryce

KELLER DRIVES UP NEXT to me just in time to see the ball I've hurled at my house bounce off a piece of wood trim, inches from the window it surrounds.

He steps down out of his truck, rubbing the back of his neck. "Damn, man. If you're just dying to have a window broken by a ball, I've got three little boys who'd be happy to take turns trying to make it happen."

"This dog's a pain in the ass. I stop what I'm doing to come out here and throw the ball so he'll quit whining at me, and he gives up after five minutes."

"In his defense, he's panting like he's been running for more than five minutes. You sure you didn't lose track of time, out here taking out your frustration on this poor clumsy dog."

"Hell if I know how long we've been out here."

"Why don't you just go to her house?"

"Because she doesn't want me there. She wants to be alone, just like she wanted last night." I retrieve the ball from the shrubs. "And she's a grown woman who has a right to decide when and if she has company."

"The night before her mom's funeral? You really think she ought to be alone right now?"

"No, Keller! I don't think she should fucking be alone right now!" I throw the ball away as hard as I can, not caring where it lands. Crash takes chase, making me look like a liar.

"Just show up. Don't ask. Let her forgive you later."

"You do know who we're talking about, right? She's never been big on forgiveness."

"She'll be gone in less than a week. You really want to waste time when you've got so little left?"

"She won't leave that soon."

"Told Catie she was."

She told me, too, but that doesn't mean she'll do it. "She'll feel different after the funeral. There are still too many decisions to be made."

"She's already signed the listing agreement to put the house on the market. Don't ask me how I know that."

As if I'd need to ask. His wife compiles data quicker than the damn CIA.

Crash spits his slobber-covered ball at my feet. My heart hammers in my chest. All I can do is stand rooted in place with my jaw clenched and my vision blurred.

Keller nods. "Figured that was knowledge I should probably share." He gets back in his truck and leaves.

Now I do want to break a window.

"You want to go for ride?" Crash runs for my truck while I lock the front door.

If she gets pissed, she can get over it. She doesn't have the first clue what she needs right now. Too stubborn for her own damn good. Leaving town in less than week. Listing the house before the funeral. The fuck is she thinking?

I change the song. Not in the mood for it. The next one's worse. Third try's no better, so I turn off the music altogether. Crash knocks his head against the window intentionally, trying to get me to roll it down for him. I lower the glass, and he leans out to let his ears flap in the wind. Not a care in the world. Lucky bastard.

Of course, there's a goddamn train! My thumb bounces on the steering wheel as I watch graffitied container cars roll past. Not one neon green dick on any of them. I laugh. "What the fuck are you doing? Are you really going to go start a fight with her the night before her mom's funeral?"

Crash pulls his head back into the cab and tilts it like he thinks I'm talking to him.

"Fuuuuuuuuuuuck!" I slam both hands into the steering wheel, accidentally honking my horn like some impatient, entitled asshole who thinks he can get a train to move faster because he has some-where important to be. Without this train forcing me to stop, I'd be on her doorstep already.

"She really shouldn't be alone though." Crash grunts like he agrees. "But if I show up unannounced, it looks like I can't re-spect her boundaries or trust her to make her own choices." His thoughtful whine is well-placed. I must be officially losing my fucking mind because I actually think I'm having a conversation with a dog. "You tell me, do I keep going or do we turn around when this train passes?"

He shakes his head. I always say he does it because he likes to hear his tags jingle on his collar, but right now, it's hard to convince myself it doesn't have some greater meaning. "No, huh? You know, your input would be a lot more helpful if I knew which option I was supposed to say no to."

I look back up at the train and wish for one of those signs from the universe people are always talking about. It probably helps to actually believe in shit like that if you expect to see it. The last train car passes, and I stare down the road at the next intersection. A red light.

"That's two signs for stop. Do I hold out for a third?" Crash is over my existential bullshit. He's got his head back out the window, ready to feel the wind again. I drive across the tracks and pull into the Quick Stop parking lot, turn around, and head back home.

She left town hating me once before. I can at least keep that from happening again.

18

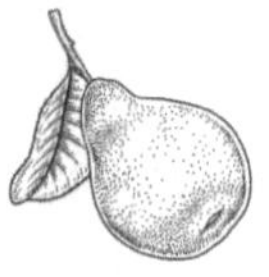

Peri

KATIE WITH A K insists on picking me up for the funeral, and no matter how unnecessary I thought it was to have someone else drive me, when I open the door and see her standing there in a hot pink pantsuit like a living Barbie, it does make me feel more at ease in my bright dress.

When she pushes her hair back to show me her peacock feather earrings, I laugh.

"How many of us will be wearing these earrings today?"

"Let's just say, there's not a pair to be had in a thirty-mile radius."

"I think we're too old to be adopting a mascot for our girl gang."

"Who told you that lie?" She leans in for a hug. "How you doing, queen?"

"Not great."

She pulls a rhinestoned flask from her purse. "Here."

"Whatever this is better not be some weird flavor. If I taste cinnamon, I'm plucking your ear feathers." I unscrew the cap and take an apprehensive sniff.

"I beg your pardon. That is top-shelf tequila."

"Well, in that case . . ." I down a swallow right there on my front porch.

"You can hang onto that."

I slip it into my purse because there was never any chance that I wasn't going to keep it.

Bryce's truck is already in the lot at Lowenstein's. Katie smiles. "You see it, right?"

"How could I miss it?" He's in the front corner spot, already positioned to be the lead car right behind the family in the procession to the cemetery. "I wonder what time he got here."

"I don't know, but I need to prepare you for something before we go in."

My grip tightens on the door handle.

"Some people are upset that there wasn't an evening viewing last night."

"The viewing is now. Mama felt it would be easier for people to just come a little earlier than to have to be here on two separate days, so that's the way I scheduled it. And she was right. It's never made sense to do it the other way. This way's better."

"I agree. It's just not the most traditional way to do it, and you know how people around here love to cling to traditions. People who can't get off work for the service, but still want to pay their respects, expect to do it at an evening viewing the night before. That's all. I don't think anyone will actually say anything to you about it, but every time I think I know something, somebody in this town surprises me." She takes my hand and gives it a squeeze. "I just didn't want you to be caught off guard."

"Goddammit! You can't win, I swear. She was thinking of everyone else with every decision she made. You know what? I wish someone would be stupid enough to express their disapproval." I gesture toward the building through the windshield. "I can't think of a more convenient place to kill somebody."

"Consult me first. It's got to look like an accident."

"Right. And you were always so good at making things look innocent, little miss obvious."

"Hey, I saved your ass more than once."

"It's a wonder I survived that whole summer you were gone."

"You must've had a guardian angel." Her eyes shift to something outside the car. "Or one extremely protective, handsome devil."

I don't have to follow her gaze to know Bryce is coming this way. Katie unlocks the doors, and he pulls mine open. "Listen," I say, turning to face him. "If I have to kill somebody today, you saw nothing."

"How could I see anything? I'm not even here." He kisses me—like planting his lips on mine in public is totally okay. "Tequila? Already?"

"She made me."

Katie laughs. "Twisted her arm until it nearly broke."

"Do y'all know you're wearing the same earrings?"

"Nothing gets by him," Katie says.

"Good thing he's on our side."

He extends his hand and I let him help me out of the car. "How many people are in there?" I ask.

"Enough to avoid anyone you need to."

"That sounds like a good number."

Katie passes me a mint. I crunch into it and hold the pieces on my tongue.

We walk inside as a united front.

And I see bright colors everywhere.

I can do this. I can do this. I can do this.

The service feels longer than it's supposed to be. I stopped listening to the words a while ago, but I'm pretty sure the preacher has disregarded my mom's request for brevity in favor of his own ego. It's freezing in here, my eyes burn from the acidic tears that won't stop leaking from them, and my nose is raw from being blown so much.

When we're finally ready to file out to head to the cemetery, I find Bryce standing just outside the door, waiting on me. "If you don't want to go in the family car, you can ride with me. I'm parked at the front. We'll be right behind them."

My Aunt Liz swoops in like a hawk and wraps her arms around my shoulders. "Marie's daughter is going in the family car."

I duck out of her grasp. "Actually, Marie's daughter is riding with him." Why can't people mind their own damn business? I had every intention of going in the family car until she butted in.

As soon as he slides behind the wheel, Bryce says, "What's with all the peacock feather earrings? Every woman we grew up with is wearing them. Does it mean something?"

"To me, it does."

"All this time I thought you liked zebras the best."

"Surprisingly, it has nothing to do with peacocks. Not really."

"Of course not."

The graveside service is short. It's a windy day, and the tent that's been set up over the chairs is about to blow away. After his closing prayer, the preacher makes the announcement I knew was coming.

"The family would like to invite everyone who wishes to join them to gather for a meal and further fellowship at the home of

Bryce Callaway. If anyone needs the address, please see a member of our staff or Mr. Callaway himself."

No, that's not right. What made him think . . . I turn in search of Bryce, but I'm met with disapproving stares from my Aunt Liz and Sandy Lindsey both. "That's not what he was supposed to say," I offer, but before I can say more, Bryce walks over to intervene.

"Lisa is at my house. The food has already been delivered. There's plenty of room for kids to roam and people to spread out. It's all handled, and your house will be clean and quiet whenever you're ready to go back to it. Nothing more to take care of today."

I never said a word to him about how much I was dreading having the house full of people again. He knew. And for once, I'm not angry that he stepped in and made a decision on my behalf. God, we used to fight about that. He always thought he knew what was best. Today, I just nod and follow him back to his truck.

Everyone shows up at his place—all my aunts and uncles, the cousins, Sandy Lindsey, even Jeannie Watts, every busybody who thinks this is just one more thing I've done wrong. They're here, anyway. And Lisa is making sure everyone has food and something to drink, a repeat performance of the way she must've been after their mom died. I know everyone came back to this house then, too. Everyone except me.

Keller has gone home and picked up Catie and the kids. Their boys apparently love Crash. They're happily throwing the ball for him while Bella shines in the newborn spotlight. I guess everybody likes to see a baby at a time like this.

A few of my friends from Houston came to the service, but they headed back home right after. I kind of wish I could've introduced them to a few of these people. Katie with a K introduced herself to them at Lowenstein's. It's no mystery how she does so well in real estate; she is still the most outgoing person I know. Extrovert doesn't begin to cover it.

I wander back inside and mingle, thank people for coming, do what is expected of me without begrudging it. When Lisa shoves a plate of finger foods into my hand, I smile and thank her. Before I know it, I've eaten it all, mindlessly snacking while making small talk.

Someone hands me a glass of water. Someone else delivers a cookie wrapped in a napkin. More hugs. More happy memories of my mom to smile and nod at. Every time I see Bryce through the crowd, he's watching me, making sure I'm okay from across the room.

People like being back in this house. They share memories of Bryce's parents and mine. Being here feels like it expands the circle, makes room for more stories, and that makes it easier for me to take a full breath, to listen because I want to, not just because I'm supposed to. I'm doing okay. Hanging in there.

My energy doesn't wane slowly; it whooshes out of me all at once. One minute, I feel like I'm coping and carrying on, and the next, I think I might hit the floor. Lisa is next to me as if I've summoned her. "Go lie down," she whispers. "It's been a long day. People will probably stick around for a while, but you've done enough."

"I don't want to be rude."

"Don't make me call my brother over here. You and I both know he will pick you up and carry you to his room, and then nobody will see either one of you until tomorrow."

I laugh, but it's too late to keep Bryce out of the equation. He's right next to me. "You need to lie down?"

"Yes," Lisa answers for me. "She does."

"I can walk myself down the hall," I warn.

"Then start walking."

We snake through the crowd to the hallway. His room is dark and cool. I sit on the edge of his bed, and he kneels down to unzip my boots. "I like this dress," he says.

"You would."

"Someday you'll have to fill me in on the meaning behind the peacock theme."

"I can't tell you that. They'll kick me out of the coven."

"You've been kicked out of everywhere else in town." We both laugh as he tucks me into his bed.

"That's not true, anymore. There are new places I haven't even been yet."

"Then you better stick around until you've checked them all off the list."

I smile because that was a good try, but I'll be gone as soon as possible. "Thank you. For everything you did today."

"Wanting to spank you feels inappropriate right now, but you've been warned more than once about thanking me for being nice to you."

"You don't care about being appropriate."

"No. But I care about you getting some rest." He kisses my forehead, and my eyes drift closed.

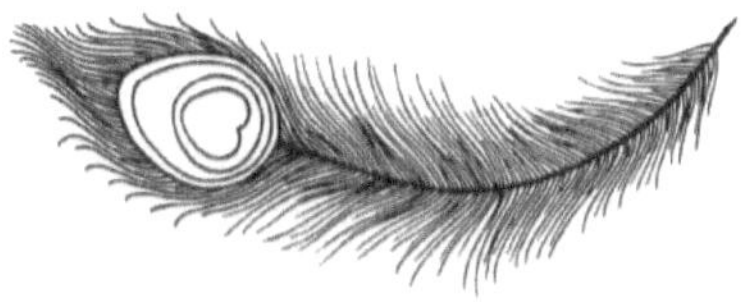

I wake to Bryce setting a cup of coffee on the nightstand next to my head. That's not late afternoon sun cutting through his blinds. It's early, which means I've been here all night. Damn. How many hours did I sleep?

"G'morn," I mumble.

"Morning. You hungry? I could make you some eggs. Or we could go out for breakfast if you want."

"I don't know." I sit up and rub my eyes. "I'm not sure what's on my to-do list today."

Someone has put my purse on the nightstand, and he hands it to me. "The first thing you need to do is get out your phone, call Katie with a K, and cancel that listing agreement."

"How do you even know about that?"

"It doesn't matter how I know. Call it off before you do something you'll regret."

"Don't start this shit, Bryce. I don't want the house. There's no sense in putting it off."

"You might want it."

"I don't."

"If you still don't want it in six months, you can sell it then."

"I'm not canceling the listing."

"Okay, first of all, it's not even that simple. It has to go through probate. Your usual way of rushing through everything isn't going to work right now. There are procedures you have to follow."

I take a deep breath. "She set up a living trust after my dad died. I am the sole heir, and I've already filed the affidavit for the deed transfer. But thank you for assuming I'm too stupid to understand the legalities."

"You're not stupid. You're just acting stupid."

I leap out of his bed and grab my boots. "I'm leaving."

"I brought you here."

"I'll get a ride."

The initial sound that leaves his mouth is a garbled exclamation, followed immediately by, "For the love of Christ, Periwinkle Eloise Abshire! Can you just calm down for five fucking minutes and listen to reason?" He's stepped closer with every word until we're toe to toe.

I gasp and glare up at him. "How dare you? You don't get to call me by my full name. The last person on earth who held that right is gone."

"Periwinkle. Eloise. Abshire. Periwinkle. Eloise. Ab—"

"Stop it, Bryce! I'm warning you!" I stare up at him, staring back down at me. He looms over me, snorting like a bull, his nostrils flared and his pupils dilated. Part of me wants nothing more than to remind him who the fuck I am, to just go at it with all I've got, but I know fighting with him isn't going to help anything. And I'm tired.

"I appreciate everything you've done to see me through losing her, and I don't know how I wouldn't have survived yesterday without you. You helped, Bryce, and I'm grateful, but I have to get back to leaning on me. As much as I'd love to put aside all the hard things to come, I learned a long time ago that hiding away and pretending the tough decisions will be easier later just makes them harder."

All at once, he deflates and takes a step back. "I'll take you home."

I step past him and head for the front door, but his hand slaps against it when I try to pull it open. "I know you won't stay, but please let me see you again. Let me be a part of your life, Pear. You can come back here sometimes, and I can come to Houston, and we can meet in the middle . . . let's just try and see what happens."

"We already know what will happen, Bryce. The nostalgia will wear off, and we'll realize we don't belong in each other's worlds anymore. Everybody has weak moments. We had ours." Crash wiggles between us and I pet his head. "Bye, buddy. You be a good boy."

"Go lay down," Bryce says, letting his hand fall away from the door.

Without hesitating, Crash lumbers off to the corner and flops onto his bed. I feel a twinge of hurt because he didn't even try to stay with me, a feeling I have no right to because he's not my dog.

Bryce won't look at me when he gets in the truck. I lean against the passenger door and wish I was already back in Houston. How did I let this get so out of hand? Weakness.

He detours onto a county road and picks up speed. *Oh, shit.* We had a nickname for this stretch in high school: Roller Coaster Road. And judging by the rest of the roads I've driven on since I've been back, I doubt the county has improved this one either. "Don't do it, Bryce."

He speeds up more. "Are you crazy? If you hit that dip going this fast, you're going to mess up your truck." He keeps going, and I rack my brain, frantically trying to remember exactly where the road drops, where we used to bottom out and catch air on the way up. But we were all driving old beaters back then. This is a brand-new pickup. His foot depresses the accelerator, and I know we're in the home stretch. I white-knuckle the door handle and squeeze my eyes shut.

I hear the siren before I open my eyes and see the lights in the side mirror. I've never been so glad to have a cop on my tail. "What are you doing? Pull over."

Ignoring me, the siren, the lights, everything but his own bull-headed determination, he keeps charging ahead. "Please stop, Bryce!" The hysteria in my voice finally gets through to him, and he brakes. We roll to a stop on the shoulder, but my heart's still racing.

Bryce rolls down his window, and an approaching voice yells, "Where the hell are you going in such a hurry, C-Way?"

"Just taking Peri home."

"Are you shitting me?" The cop's face comes into view.

"Mikey? You're a cop now?"

"Hey, girl. I'm sorry about your mom."

"You're a cop?" I ask again. "I smoked my first joint with you."

Bryce's head snaps in my direction. "Do what? When did you and Maltsberger hang out?"

"You always remember your first," Mike jokes, but he flashes an entirely unnecessary cocky grin my way. His timing really couldn't be any worse with that shit. Bryce is already high-strung and spoiling for a fight.

"The fuck did he mean by that?" Bryce is staring lasers at me.

"Are you serious right now? You knew you weren't my first. Not like I was yours either."

"All this time I assumed your first was Granger. He was the only boyfriend I ever knew you had before me. How did I miss that you dated Maltsberger?"

"We didn't exactly date." I shrug.

Mike lets out a long, low whistle. "Damn, I'm sorry." The smirk on his face makes clear he's not. "I thought the statute of limitations had run out on that secret."

Bryce turns his head slowly to face Mike. Too slowly. Menacingly slow. And then he spits right on his badge.

Oh, hell. How is this my life?

"I don't think you want to do this, Callaway."

"Yeah? Well, I bet this ain't the first time you've been wrong."

"Why don't you step out of the truck and talk to me for a minute?"

"Yes, sir, Officer Maltsberger." Bryce flings his door open. His boots hit the gravel. And he swings.

"Nooooo!" Before the scream can fully leave my mouth, his fist makes contact with Mike's jaw, and I scramble across the seat and leap out to jump between them.

Mike rubs his jaw. Bryce's fist is still clenched, and I swear his body is vibrating like a live wire. "What the hell is wrong with you?" I yell. "You just assaulted a police officer, you fucking moron! I can't free the zebras, but you can pull this shit?"

"You and Maltsberger? And you never once thought to mention that?"

"I never mentioned it because it was none of your business!"

"Everything about you was my business!"

"No, it wasn't! You didn't own me, Bryce!"

"I never tried to own you. Nobody could've ever fucking owned you. Just trying to love you was like trying to bottle lightning!"

"I'm sorry I was so hard to love!"

"Well, you were. You were damn hard to love sometimes, Peri. But you are goddamn impossible to unlove." He shoves me against the truck and kisses me, hard and angry.

And I kiss him back with the same ferocity. His energy feels like he's succeeded in bottling lightning, like he could explode and incinerate the whole world right now. And I'm matching him volt for volt, and there's no denying what's crackling in the air between us and around us—the anger and the hurt and the inevitability of us burning it down all over again. I've been telling myself the way we still make each other feel is a mirage built on memories, but the heat and need and desperation of this moment is as real as it's ever been.

Mike clears his throat behind us. "Um, hey, I hate to interrupt this little roadside honeymoon, but . . ."

We pull apart and look at him. "I ought to take you to jail right now, C-Way."

Bryce stands up straight and juts his wrists forward like he's daring Mike to cuff him. Men and their pissing contests, I swear. Mike shakes his head. "But what I'm going to do instead is watch you turn your truck around, and then I'm going to follow you back to your house to be sure you park it. And you're going to go inside and not put your hands on the wheel again until you've cooled off. Deal?"

"No," I say. "He has to take me home first."

A growl emanates from Bryce's chest. Mike throws his hands up. "Fine. I'll follow him to your house where he can park his truck, and then he can stay there until he cools off."

"It's the law," Bryce says. "We have to spend the rest of the day together."

"Won't be the first law you've broken," I say.

"Yeah, but I behave when I'm under surveillance."

"It's true," Mike says. "I'll be watching."

Bryce grins. "Your place or mine?"

"Mine, so I can at least change out of this awful dress."

"I like that dress," both men say in unison. Bryce flexes like he might take another swing, and I sigh.

"Take me home."

Mike leaves the flashing lights on the whole way just to fuck with Bryce. As we're walking inside, he hits the siren for a few seconds before he drives off.

"Asshole," we both say.

"Really, though? Maltsberger?"

"Not that it's any of your business, but it was one time."

"Your first time."

"And every time after was with you."

"You're right. This dress is terrible. You should take it off immediately."

19

Bryce

THE MOMENT PERI UNTIES the string on the side of her dress, and it falls open to reveal the lace of another matching bra-and-panty set, anything she's done with anybody else, before me or since, becomes meaningless. When she unties the inside string, my hands go to her waist while she shrugs out of the dress completely.

I kiss her neck and whisper an apology. "I'm sorry. For everything, the things I did wrong, the things that went wrong without warning, I'm just so damn sorry for all of it."

She rolls her head back, and her hair still smells sweet, despite the outside air blowing through it at the cemetery yesterday and today on the side of the road. Her hands find my shoulders and I can feel the heat of her skin through my shirt.

"I told myself years ago that I was done with all that," she says. "That I wouldn't spend another second wondering why or what if. I let it all go right then and there. But the moment I saw you grumbling over those chickens, it felt like someone had kicked an ant bed in my stomach. I really believed I was done . . ." Her voice cracks. "And then I thought if I could just remember how to be angry at you again, but when I got close enough to breathe the same air, I knew I'd forgotten too well."

I pull her body firmly against mine and hold on like the world might suddenly accelerate and spin us apart. "It didn't take me long to remind you."

She laughs into my chest, and I pick her up and carry her down the hall.

When I lower her to the bed, she reaches behind her back to unhook her bra. I pull my shirt over my head while she takes her panties down her legs. And then she slides off the bed onto her knees right in front of me and uses both her hands to unbuckle my belt. I let her unbutton and unzip my jeans, and watch as she pulls them down my thighs along with my underwear. The tip of my hard cock brushes her cheek, and my spine jolts.

She runs the tip of her tongue up the length of my dick, maintaining eye contact with me as she does it. So many things we've done hundreds of times before feel like firsts between us. They are firsts for the man and woman we are now.

Her eyes are red-rimmed and swollen, but her glassy green irises hold me in an intense stare as she laves the head, working her way closer to the tip, ultimately licking the pre-cum from it, and then teasingly flicking her tongue over the seam a few times.

She's undeniably beautiful, but her confidence has always been endlessly sexy to me. I've never met a woman who could hold a candle to the girl I remembered. And the woman she's become makes me feel like I'm still that wildly infatuated boy, but every bit a grown man.

The way she's taking her time, giving me nothing more than feathery touches of her tongue, letting my anticipation build, has me moaning and my eyelids fluttering. She takes the crown fully into her mouth, and the feeling nearly takes my knees.

Our eye contact is broken by the dip of her head as she sinks down to push me to the back of her throat. My hands sink into her hair, and she glides her mouth slowly up until the tip is all that remains inside, and then slowly back down again until I'm nearly fully sheathed in her hot, soft mouth. She repeats the actions a few times, and then she pulls off until her mouth completely separates from my dick, letting her saliva spill from her mouth before she resumes, hollowing her cheeks and bobbing her head faster now.

I could come in her mouth, but I need this to be more, to give her more.

Using my hands in her hair, I pull her up. She winces as she rises to face me, but there's ecstasy in her expression.

This is her release now, not running wild and pushing boundaries out in the world, but having her physical boundaries pushed in private. I want to explore this in so many ways, ways that require conversations I don't want to pause to have right now.

But soon, soon I want to ask questions and learn about all her changes that evolved while I wasn't around to see them happening. Shifts I didn't get to experience. Seems improbable that we could have so many new things in common, things that emerged when we were so far removed from each other, but I'm fairly certain we do.

Her kisses are frenzied and erotic. My hands can't touch her in enough places at once. We fall to the bed, and I draw her nipple into my mouth. She drags her fingernails up the back of my neck, sending a chill across my shoulders as her hands continue up into my hair.

Her hips roll against mine. "Fuck me."

With my boots still on and my jeans at my knees, I sink my cock into the welcoming heat. "You are so fucking tight." Her pussy gushes when I praise her body. She was already incredibly wet, but I'll never get enough of her soaking the sheets for me. "That's my girl. I love feeling this sweet little snatch squeezing me."

"God, your dick feels good."

"Your perfect little wet pussy feels incredible. I think it's missed my cock."

"For so long, I wanted to know what you'd be like now." She makes sure we have eye contact before she goes on. "What you'd think of the way I am now."

"I am so very into the way you are." I kiss her again. "I want us to sit down later and talk about everything you like, but tell me what you want right now, so I can give it to you."

"Hold me down and tell me what I am when I let you dominate me and use me."

I pin her wrists and slam my hips forward, driving balls-deep into her. She sucks in a breath as if I've forced it from her lungs. "Such a good little whore, taking all that dick. Do you like taking it all at once?"

"Yes. I love the way it feels when your cock stretches me inch by inch, but I love when you fill me hard and fast, too."

My core clenches, and a groan churns up through my chest. "Your tender little cunt got creamy when you said that. I wonder why that happened." I bite just above her collar bone.

"Because it's a slutty little cunt."

"For who?"

"You."

"For me? This slutty little cunt is all mine?"

"Yes. Yes." Her breathing stutters. "Oh, God."

"Yeah, that's a good girl, showing Daddy what his greedy little cock-hungry whore likes." I know using the word Daddy is risky when we haven't talked about it, but I had a hunch, and her spasming pussy is proving it true. "Come for me, baby. Milk my cock, so I can come inside you." I drop my mouth to suck on her nipple again, and she quakes under me, straining like she wants to free her wrists, but she doesn't use her word, so I don't loosen my grip. My balls get tight, and my dick lurches as she thrashes under me while I pound into her. Her breathing morphs to the short shrieks I love to hear as she pants her way through her orgasm.

My spine stiffens, locking my neck and shoulders, and the toes of my boots dig into her comforter as my cock empties in her silken walls. She is fucking perfection.

I release her wrists while I catch my breath. She rolls her hands from side to side when I free them.

"I didn't hurt you, did I?"

"No. But your grip is strong. You should invest in fur-lined cuffs before you injure some poor fragile woman."

All the oxygen leaves the room at her casual reference to some hypothetical other woman whose wrists I don't want to hold. "I keep those at home."

"And you didn't pull them out for me? Now I'm hurt."

"You keep giving me visions of you in handcuffs and I will go buy some."

She plays with the hair behind my ear. "I still can't believe Mikey's a cop. Or that you punched him."

"I still can't believe you gave him your virginity."

"Why do men have to talk about it like that? Like it's some priceless gift. It's the most bumbling, confusing sexual encounter anyone has."

"It's not just men. There are some women who think it's a pretty special occasion."

"I know, but it fascinates me how people build it up into this magical moment, when the truth is most of us just decide we're ready to get it over with." She shakes her head. "God, maybe there's always been something wrong with me."

"There has never been anything wrong with you. And there's nothing wrong with you now."

"For the record, what we just did . . . that felt bigger than losing my v-card."

"It was a pretty big thing to share. I'm glad we went there, but I may have torn your comforter with my boots. I'll buy you a new one."

"Don't worry about it. One less thing to have to donate."

"If you sell this house, you're going to have to stay with me every time you come to town to see Katie and Catie."

"And you think I'm going to be doing a lot of that?"

"You'll try to say you're coming to see them, but I'll know you're really coming to see me."

"Oh, you'll know, huh?"

I collapse next to her and pull her into my side. "Daddy always knows."

She laughs and rolls her eyes. "You were only Daddy in the heat of the moment."

"No. You might only call me that in the heat of the moment but—"

"Uh, fact check. I didn't call you that. You called yourself that."

"Yeah, but you liked it. Do you want to call me Daddy?"

I feel her pull away. Her body doesn't move an inch but it just took back every ounce of openness she'd let loose. *Fuck. I pushed her too far.* I stroke her arm, close my eyes, and enjoy her softness. Every time I turn around, I need to apologize for something else.

Wanting to take things slow and being able to are not the same.

20

Peri

KATIE WITH A K shows up minutes after Bryce leaves my house. I have to give her credit for not ringing the doorbell before he left. Something tells me she drove around the block a few times. Call it intuition. Or it could be the way she's chewing her lip like she's dying to say something, but she wants to wait for the right moment so it has the most impact.

"Did you come to retrieve your dime-store-cowgirl flask?"

"No, you can take that back to Houston, so you have something to remember me by. I don't want you to forget me again."

"I never forgot you." I hold the door open to invite her in. "I'd be willing to bet no one ever has."

"Speaking of unforgettable . . ."

Here it comes.

"It's adorable how y'all are doing one night at his place and one night at yours now."

"I fell asleep at his after the funeral and slept until morning. And then when he was driving me home, we got pulled over by Mikey Maltsberger—and can we just talk about how desperate this town must be for police officers to have hired his crazy ass—but anyway, after Bryce punched him in the face, Officer Mikey said if he didn't want to go to jail, he had to park his truck for the rest of the day, and that's how it ended up in my driveway overnight again."

"That is the most Peri and Bryce story I have heard in a long, long time."

"Well, we figured y'all could use some new material."

"Why the hell would Bryce punch Mikey? They've been friends since elementary school. As far as I know, they've never had a problem."

"That secret I was going to take to my grave? Mike felt the time had come to share it."

"Hold up. Let me get this straight. He pulls Bryce over, walks up to the truck, sees you, says hey, Peri, sorry about your mom, but oh, by the way, bro, I popped her cherry?"

"It was pretty much exactly like that."

"And then Bryce just bailed out and punched him?"

"To be honest, I'm a little fuzzy on the details. It all happened so fast, and I was still processing Mike's spontaneous confession, but basically, yeah."

"Holy shit. It's true. They never grow up."

"Apparently, not entirely, no."

"Well, I hope you and Bryce at least had a good night?"

As hard as I try to hold back my telling smile, it spreads across my face like I'm part Cheshire Cat.

"Oh, it must've been a very good night."

"Whatever. I think he felt like he had something to prove."

"And did he prove it?"

"Is this what you came over here for this morning? Or does it have something to do with that?" I nod at the envelope in her hand.

"The appraiser was in the neighborhood yesterday, so he swung by to take a preliminary look at the outside of the house. He dropped this note at my office to give us a heads up that his final report will require a roof inspection. He's recommending a new roof and feels sure the inspector will say the same."

"Fuck him. New roof. Just give me whatever addendum I need to sign to sell it as is."

"It doesn't work like that, Peri. If the appraisal is subject to a new roof or repairs, they have to be done."

"Let's use a different appraiser. This guy obviously has a stick up his ass."

"You can't choose your appraiser. They're assigned. The only reason I have this information already is because it's Antonio."

"Segovia? Dammit, I knew I should've gone out with him when he asked."

"Right. So Bryce would have somebody else to punch." She laughs. "The good news is the inside of the house is in great shape. You shouldn't have any more surprises."

"Should I just go ahead and schedule the new roof now?"

"You can wait on the full appraisal to come in, but the appointment for him to look at the inside isn't until next week, and then you'll have to wait on the inspector, and hope he only calls for repairs."

"All I'm hearing from that is more time, more time, more time. I'm probably going to have to spend the money, anyway. Give me a recommendation for a roofer."

"You knew we couldn't sell it overnight. The title commitment's going to take at least a week, and that's with me calling in a favor. But to answer your question, yes, I'd go ahead and do the new roof if I were in your shoes."

"Thanks. Can you get me a name?"

She waggles the envelope. "I've included three in case you want to get bids."

"Bids. Yeah, I didn't think about that. Again, thank you."

"This is typical stuff, I promise. Everything will work out fine."

I know she means everything with the house, but my brain hears it as everything-everything, and I exhale a little more at the comfort that brings.

"Whenever you're ready to pack up her stuff, you know I'll help. I can hang out this morning if you need me."

"I appreciate it, but I need to shower and sort through some mental stuff before I tackle anything else."

Katie leaves me with the roofer recommendations and my thoughts. The house is quiet, and the urge to sit on the couch and stare at the wall until I'm catatonic is strong, but when I sit still for too long, it all catches up to me.

I turn the shower dial to the left for the second time, increasing the heat until steam starts to rise around me. Breathing the steam helps clear my sinuses. I forget I'm not used to all this pollen anymore. Bracing my hands on the wall, I close my eyes and inhale.

The memory of Bryce putting me in the shower invades my head immediately. Him washing my hair and my body . . . I thought I was doing fine until he took over and made that one simple decision for me. He knew I needed a hot shower, and to be taken care of, more than I needed to fight him in that moment. There's nobody else alive anymore who knows me like that.

I'm rationalizing, making things out to be more meaningful than they are. Or worse, I'm taking advantage of his feelings for me, leading him on because it feels good to escape with him.

How could he possibly think we could be in a relationship at this point in our lives? I can give him a list a mile long of reasons that's a terrible idea: One, I live in Houston and he lives here. Two . . . fuck, it just wouldn't work. He still thinks it's okay to throw his fists the moment his ego gets thumped.

And I'm a grown woman, who doesn't act on impulse anymore. Dirty karaoke notwithstanding. Or the fact that I followed him home from H-E-B to make him a sandwich and get naked in his kitchen five minutes after seeing him for the first time in eight years. Jesus wept! What is wrong with me?

I don't have a single friend in Houston who even knows Bryce Callaway's name. I don't talk about him, don't even bring him up after a few drinks. Never. When I'm there, he's so far in my past I have to make an effort to find those memories. But here, I feel his touch long after he's gone, constantly hear his voice, see his face when I close my eyes, feel the comfort of his arms . . . he's everywhere. He's is in this shower with me right now, rising in the steam like a genie, just waiting for me to make my next wish so he can grant it on demand—

Fuckity, fuck, fuck, fuck! I slam my palm against the shower knob to turn off the water.

Wrapped in a towel that my mom probably bought twenty years ago—because until it reached the point of being completely unusable, she didn't replace anything—I leave the bathroom and stand in the cool hallway for a minute to catch my breath. The steam that was supposed to make it easier to breathe ended up nearly choking me.

My feet start to move toward her room instead of mine. Pausing for one more deep breath, I open the door. It's not good to keep rooms closed off. They get musty. And when doors stay closed for too long, they stick sometimes, don't want to reopen.

I step across the threshold, expecting to feel her in some way—the love, the loss, something to take the place of all the things I felt in the shower.

But the room is an emotional void. I thought walking in here for the first time after her death would be a momentous thing, but it's just space. I sit in the recliner still positioned next to her bed and pull my feet up under me. She's gone, so completely and totally gone. I know she'll never be gone from my thoughts or my heart, all that sentimental crap I'm supposed to find solace in. I won't be able to banish her memories the way I did Bryce's for so long, and I'd never want to, but I didn't know she could be so tangibly gone so quickly.

The blanket I always kicked off my lap before I fell asleep in here is still bunched at my side. I spread it across my body and sink down into the cushion. I'm drained, but I know this is the only place I'm going to be able to fall asleep right now. I can't make decisions today, or take phone calls or messages. Not yet.

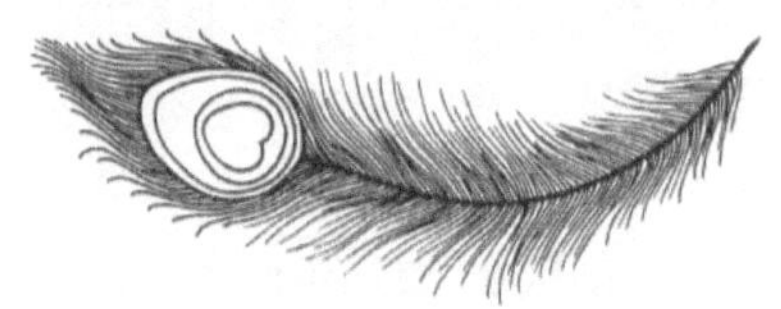

My foot lifts immediately off the cold kitchen tiles when I take my first step onto them. I need to turn the air off, maybe even turn the heat on. Backtracking to my room, I put on socks and a sweatshirt. The state of my hair is hilarious in the mirror, but only because I'm the only one here to see it. I'd hide under the bed before I'd let anyone see it like this. That's what I get for falling asleep in a chair while it was wet.

Fuzzy socks make the kitchen tiles bearable while I rummage through the containers in the freezer. There are some smaller, single-serving sizes. Some people really are incredibly thoughtful.

I'm not resentful anymore toward everyone who came and brought food, but there's still way too much of it here. And none of it sounds appetizing. Nothing piques my interest at all until I find a small container of bread pudding. I zap it in the microwave and grab a bag of Fritos Scoops from the counter. I need some salty with my sweet, and these can double as spoons so they're an efficient choice. And there's nobody here to judge me.

I take my snacks to the couch and settle in with some reality TV. Katie with a K calls right when I'm about to find out why the bosun is being called into the captain's quarters. He needs to be sent home after what he did. I'd send him home. I am way too invested in this shit. "Hey, don't worry. I haven't set the place on fire for the insurance money."

Katie laughs. "What are you doing?"

"Eating bread pudding on Fritos Scoops."

"Why?"

"Because they're like little spoons."

"That doesn't begin to answer my question, but when you're done with that, grab the box from the funeral home and come to Catie and Keller's house."

"Now it's my turn to ask why."

"Because there should be packets of thank you cards in there, along with the cards from all the flower arrangements, and we're going to help you fill them out. There's also a notebook on the dining room table that has a list of everyone who brought food and their addresses."

I'd seen the notebook on the table. "Y'all don't have to do that."

I hear Catie with a C yell in the background. "Let us help, Peri! Come over!"

"All you do is write the same message again and again," Katie says. "It's no big deal. Besides, all three of us haven't gotten to spend any time together because Catie was too pregnant to do anything, and now she has a new little semen demon attached to her every two hours, so bring your ass over here and hang out with us."

Only Katie with a K could get away with calling somebody's newborn baby a semen demon right in front of them. She's married, but no kids in her future. She never wanted kids, and she somehow found a man who shares her goal to remain childless and can handle her brash intensity. If I'm being honest, I kind of want to meet this unicorn husband of hers before I leave town.

I run a wet comb through my hair and pull it back into a ponytail. It's definitely still in no shape to leave the house without a ball cap. Adding jeans and a bra under the sweatshirt is all I can manage toward making myself presentable. We won't be going anywhere, so it doesn't really matter what I look like, but it's not my most photogenic day.

The box from the funeral home is on the dining room table next to the notebook. I grab both on my way out.

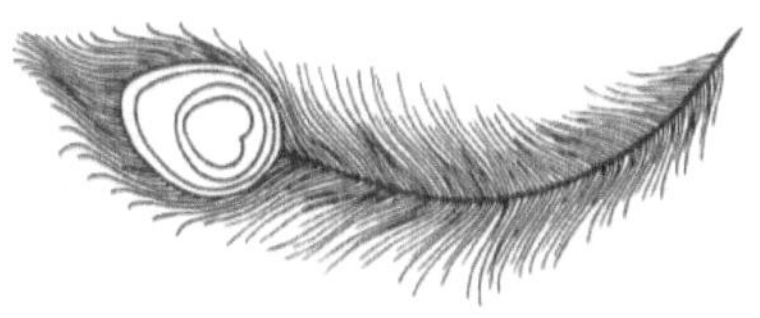

The terrible trio rushes out to greet me again. "Do you remember our names?" Easton asks.

"Of course, I do. It would be impossible to forget them." I don't share my reason. "You're Easton. And you're Weston. And you're just Tyson." Okay, these boys are entirely too cute. Those little smiles are priceless. All because I knew their names.

I walk in to find Katie and Catie at the kitchen table, one with a glass of wine in her hand and the other with a baby attached to her boob again. "Why would you drink in front of someone who can't?" I don't mean to sound so accusatory, but it seems insensitive, even for Katie.

Katie looks like I just asked her to solve the energy crisis. "Because I'm not a walking food source so I can."

Catie laughs. "It's fine. I don't mind, I promise. Have a glass."

Well, shit. Apparently, I'm insensitive, too, because she doesn't have to tell me twice. I drop the box and the notebook on the table, and notice Catie already has three pens laid out for us. "Do you really think we should fill them out with purple pens?"

"We never used anything but purple pens in high school," she says, laughing as she shifts Bella up to her shoulder. "I couldn't resist. People won't care what color the ink is."

"She's right," Katie agrees. "Pour your wine, come sit down, and tell us all about the hot sex you're having with the love of your life."

Catie nods like a kid saying yes to a cupcake. "Keller refuses to pump Bryce for info, so you better start sharing all the dirty details." She pats the baby's back.

"We were high school sweethearts, not the love of each other's lives. And no, I'm not spilling any recent details, especially not with little ears around."

"Boys, go outside!" Catie yells.

I laugh. "Nice try."

"Keller and I were high school sweethearts, too. Look at us now."

"I don't want to marry Bryce and have five kids."

"We only have four."

"So far," Katie says.

"I think you should share about your own life," I say, turning to Katie. "How'd you meet a guy from somewhere else and convince him to move back home to Copper with you?"

"Are you kidding? Derek loves it here. It was his idea to live in Copper."

"Is this man hiding from the FBI?"

"I don't think Derek has ever broken a rule in his life, let alone a law."

"Okay, now I have so many more questions. How did you even end up together?"

"He thought I was fun. I thought he was the nicest guy I'd ever met. We were both right."

Catie nods. "She's not kidding. They're sickeningly perfect together."

"Well, I think you both deserve sickeningly perfect. Cheers!"

I open the box and divvy up the thank you cards and the cards from the florists. Catie pushes a pen toward each of us. "What about you?" she asks. "Anybody come close to perfect over the years?"

"She means close to Bryce," Katie clarifies.

"Thanks for that entirely unnecessary translation. And the answer is no. The closest I came to settling down was with a chef I dated for a little over a year. He'd just opened his third restaurant, and all of a sudden, he decided it was time to get married, and he just assumed I'd agree. I wanted to keep things the way they were. He didn't, so that was the end of that."

"Do you ever see him around?"

"No, and I intentionally don't go to any of his restaurants anymore. It was a couple years ago. For all I know, he found somebody else to marry by now."

"Hmmm," Katie with a K says, thoughtfully. "I always thought I might like saying, 'yes, chef.'"

"Well, I never did, so . . ." I open a card and start writing.

"You and Bryce were pretty dirty for a high school couple," Catie with a C says, her big blue eyes daring me to confirm or deny the claim. "How compatible are y'all these days? I know you're not looking to rekindle any forever hopes and dreams, but physically, was it awkward to be with him after so long?"

"It was very much *not* awkward."

"His skills still get the job done, huh?" Katie goes to the counter to refill her wine glass.

"I think it would be rare for someone's sexual prowess to fade in their twenties, Katie."

"Yeah, but things change. People change," she says. "I thought Connor and I were pretty hot together back then, but I can't imagine trying to date him again at this age."

"I'm sure Connor has learned some new tricks since he was eighteen."

Bella burps, and Catie rocks in her chair while writing at the same time. That must be some multitasking magic that comes with motherhood. "What I just heard you say was Bryce has new tricks. Keep talking."

"Shutting up entirely now."

"Oh, no you're not," Katie says, topping off my wine. "Listen, you were the only girl I knew back then whose boyfriend was using her tights to tie her to a headboard in his aunt's lake house. So, been tied up since you've been back in town?"

"Sorry to disappoint you, but the answer is no." It's not a lie. Having my wrists restrained in his hands isn't the same thing. It's better. Way hotter. And I'm not mentioning it in this kitchen. But now that she's brought up the tights and the lake house, I'm thinking it probably only makes sense that Bryce and I both like the things we like now. I guess seventeen was a little younger than average to hop on the bondage train. Wow. Some things never seem weird until you hear someone else say it out loud over a decade later.

"The crazy shit you and Bryce used to dare each other to do," Catie says. "And the pranks y'all pulled on each other."

Katie shakes her pen, scribbles on the edge of the notebook to get the ink flowing. "Remember, when you duct-taped the doors of his truck shut while he was at football practice? I still don't know how no one saw you in the parking lot."

"How was I supposed to know it would take the paint off when he removed it? God, I was so scared when my dad told me Mr. Callaway said I had to pay to have the truck repainted. I cried for hours in my room before my mom came in and told me my dad had been teasing me. Mr. Callaway thought it was funny, said it was nothing but an old work truck, anyway."

"Bryce didn't think it was funny. Remember how he'd get all puffed up when he got mad back then?" Catie with a C does her best imitation of his mad face, and we all laugh.

"He still does that. He loved that old truck, though. But I didn't think it was funny when he stole my steering wheel so I'd have to ride home from that party with him either."

"It was the only way he could get you to talk to him." Leave it to Katie with a K to defend him on that one.

"And y'all jumped ship and found other rides and left me stuck with him. Anyway, the joke was on him. I was silent the whole way home."

"You were so damn stubborn."

"So was he."

"Some of us have to find our complete opposite to balance us," Katie says. "But I can't imagine you ever being happy with someone who couldn't match you, step for step."

"I am happy, though. Not so much right now, but I will be again. I like my life."

"And you don't like what you're doing here with Bryce?" Catie leans back to check on her boys in the other room, but when her eyes turn back to me, she stares like I've agreed to a lie detector test and she's the machine.

"Who doesn't like having great sex?" I ask, careful to keep my voice low.

"So, it's great. Okay, now we're talking."

"No, we're not."

We work our way through all the thank you cards. I can't believe how long it took with three of us, and I can't imagine how long it would've taken me to do them alone. Of course, I wouldn't have stopped every few minutes to interrogate myself about Bryce.

Keller comes home with pizza, and the boys mob him. He settles them in the dining room, and then he drops a box in the center of the kitchen table, flips open the lid, and says, "Here, I got y'all this crime against pizza."

It's loaded with feta cheese and pineapple and it smells amazing. "Aw, every time I start to think I might leave you, you do something right."

He laughs and kisses Catie, and then Bella. They really are still damn cute together. "Thanks, Keller. Please swing by the house and take some more food out of the freezer. I can't possibly eat all that before I leave."

His eyebrows lift. "And when's that going to be?"

"Few more days probably. The house needs a new roof, apparently. So, I've got to get that at least scheduled."

"I'll tell Bryce to grab whatever you don't want the next time he's over there." He doesn't give me time for a rebuttal before he goes back to check on the boys and eat with them.

Katie grabs a chunk of warm pineapple and pops it into her mouth. "You probably want to stick around until the new roof is on, to make sure it gets done right."

"As long as it passes inspection, I don't care how they do it, and I wouldn't know if it was being done right, anyway."

"No, but you'll know that they're using the shingles you picked out, and that they're showing up."

"I trust my realtor. I know she'll make sure it gets done right. Are the boys in any activities yet, Catie?"

"Second year of t-ball coming up. And Easton just started kindergarten, so that's been an adjustment."

"Whoa. I didn't even think about him being old enough for school." The disparities between our lives is mind-blowing, but I feel comfortable at her kitchen table. It's been nice to spend an afternoon with them, even with all the Team Bryce stuff.

"Well, you're not leaving before we all have dinner together at my house." Katie says it as if it's already been decided, the way she says everything. "I want you to meet Derek. And Catie and Keller need to get out of the house for a few hours. Her mom will watch the kids." Again, she's making all the plans for everyone. "And I like seeing you and Bryce together, so you can indulge me one last time before you run away again."

"The difference is I won't be running away this time, Katie. I'll just be heading back home. But I'd love to meet Derek, so count me in."

I gather my box and notebook, and hug them goodbye. I pause at the dining room. "Bye, boys."

They all wave and shout their goodbyes while their dad stares at me. "Don't look at me like that, Keller." I turn on my heels and head for the front door.

"He punched a cop for you!" he yells.

I laugh without looking back. "He punched that cop for himself, and you know it."

As I step outside, I hear one of the boys says, "I want to punch a cop!"

Oh, Catie with a C. I don't envy you, but I'm so glad you're happy.

21

Bryce

FRIDAY NIGHT DINNER AT Katie with a K's house wouldn't normally get me excited. I wouldn't normally have said yes to the invitation, or been invited to begin with. She set this up as a couples' dinner, and Peri said she wants to go. Supposedly, she said yes because she wants to meet Katie's husband.

I've met the guy enough times to know he's not much for talking, not that we'd have much to talk about. He doesn't drink beer, only scotch. Golfs, but mostly for the networking, whatever the fuck that means. Wears boots, but not work boots. He claims he was born and raised in Texas, but he comes off sort of Texas-adjacent. It's not just me; Keller gets the same vibe from the guy.

Peri agreed to let me pick her up, too. Letting a man pick her up and drive her to dinner is a date. Period. And we're going to a couples-only dinner party. So, that makes us a couple, at least for a few hours. Even she can't deny that.

Standing on her front porch, waiting for the door to be opened, still makes me nervous. There's no chance her dad is going to open it and shake my hand with a smile on his face while simultaneously sending the message with his eyes that I'll never be good enough for his daughter. Her mom won't welcome me inside and immediately ask what our plans are for the evening. It'll be Peri. And she'll take my breath away just like she does every time I see her.

She steps outside in a rush, and her perfume wraps around us as she turns to lock the door. "Why are you in such a hurry?"

"We're supposed to be there at six."

"It's only 5:45."

"It takes longer than fifteen minutes to get there."

I shrug. "Maybe twenty at the most. I don't think they're going to lock us out."

Her eyes cut toward mine. Her makeup is perfect, but it's obvious she's been crying today. I hug her without saying a word because I don't want to risk upsetting her again. "You look beautiful."

"You're a terrible liar, but you smell nice."

"So do you. And you look beautiful."

"You gonna hug me on this porch all night or take me to dinner?"

"I never imagined I'd be almost thirty and still picking you up from this house for a date."

She pulls away and laughs. "This is not a date."

"Oh, it's a date."

"Then where are my roses?"

"It's not a first date."

"I don't recall you bringing me flowers on our first date either."

"So, I owe you roses, huh?"

"I don't make the rules."

"You've always made your own rules."

"You never let me make yours, though."

"Nope." I kiss her on the forehead before I open the truck door for her. "But I'll buy you roses voluntarily. Some day when you're not even expecting them."

Katie opens her door and welcomes us with a judgmental scowl. "Keller and Catie made it on time, and they have five kids."

"Four!" Catie yells from another room.

"So far," I say as we walk in.

"They have a curfew," Peri says. "We don't. You'll never get rid of us."

Derek comes into view. "Welcome." He shakes my hand and introduces himself to Peri. "I've heard so much about you. It's a pleasure to finally meet you."

"I'm sure you're already aware, but your wife exaggerates," Peri says.

We all laugh and follow Katie into the living room. When the timer goes off on the oven, I think we've already shocked the shit out of Derek with our glory days stories.

Halfway through dinner, he looks up at Katie and says, "I didn't realize every girl you grew up with was just like you."

Catie with a C points her knife at him. "You take that back. I'm not above shanking you in your own dining room."

"They weren't all like us," Katie says. "We were special."

Keller nods and lifts his glass. "To Peri and the Caties."

"You better have spelled that with a C in your head," Catie says.

Everybody called them that back in high school. And Catie and Katie always argued over how it should be spelled. Peri tried spelling it as CKaties, but they just argued over which letter should come first and whether it should be pronounced as See Katies or Kay Katies.

The stories keep progressing through high school, and my stomach knots, thinking ahead to the final crazy story, the one that made Peri leave and stay gone. I don't think anybody will intentionally bring it up, but sometimes people start reminiscing and talk about things before they think. I've had to deal with it more than once. It's entertaining as hell for everybody else.

Makes me want to go back in time and kick the shit out of myself. I was a dumbass eighteen-year-old, who had no idea how far that would go or that there would be an official investigation.

I look up to catch Katie looking at me like she knows what I'm thinking. "Who wants dessert?" she says to interrupt the current story.

While she's in the kitchen, slicing a pie, Keller and Catie explain the "neon green dick" that's been referenced half a dozen times tonight, right down to me and Peri getting arrested for it. That one's still funny.

"I hate that the mural's gone," Peri says. "Those new owners suck. It makes me want to paint a neon green dick on their building even without the hands."

"I'll buy the spray paint," Keller says with a hint of dare in his voice.

His wife kills the notion. "You can't afford spray paint. I already spent all your money on diapers this week."

It's not like we'd actually go recreate the legendary graffiti, but it's fun to talk about it like any of us might still be young and dumb enough.

Derek's not as stiff as I'd thought before. He's pretty witty once he gets going. I kind of understand him and Katie better now. And if there is one person here tonight who might actually take off for the brick wall at Crawford's with a can of spray paint at the ready, it's his wife. She needs this guy. I forget sometimes that Peri wasn't the only one of them who was wild and impulsive.

The CKaties still live here, so I see them as adults, forget about the girls they once were sometimes. But Peri is forever that impetuous girl in my mind. I can't imagine ever not seeing her that way first.

As soon as Keller eats his last bite of pie, Catie says they have to go. We all protest, but she says, "I didn't bring my breast pump because I didn't think we'd be gone long enough for me to need it. But it's that time, so we have no choice."

Keller opens his mouth to say something, but she puts her hand across it. "Do not ruin a perfectly nice night. I'm begging you."

Peri and I stick around for a while after they've gone. Derek asks about her work, and I enjoy listening to her share about her job. We haven't talked much about it. I tune out a little when she happily talks about her life in Houston outside of work. Self-preservation. I'm glad she's happy, but it stings to see her face light up like that and not be a part of it.

When he asks me how business is going, and I mention the guys I've hired, Peri looks at me in shock. "I didn't realize you had full-time employees. I thought they were temporary, just to help with that big job."

"No, I plan to keep them on. I really should've hired somebody sooner, but I wanted to hold out until I had no choice."

"Wow . . ." Her voice trails off, and our eyes meet. The reality of how tied in place we both are—me here and her there—hits me hard. She feels it, too. I know she does.

22

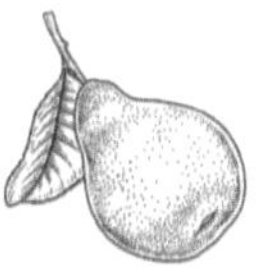

Peri

WE STAY WAY LATER than I thought we would at Katie and Derek's. It was fun, and I'm glad we all got together like that. Bryce seems restless as we head out of their neighborhood. "You want to go to Jolene's?" he asks.

"Yeah, sure," I say. "But we don't have to go to the wine bar. We can go somewhere else. Freeloaders' or Krazy Kactus, wherever."

"Wherever we go, we're likely to run into people we grew up with. Do you want to run into them in a bar where they'll ask you to dance over and over again or—"

"Jolene's is good. But no karaoke."

"Katie would never forgive us if we did that without her there."

"She'd probably be mad if she knew we were going there at all without her," I say.

"If you want to invite them, you can."

"No. I think I'd rather go with just you."

"I'm never going to complain about getting to have you all to myself."

I should warn him not to read anything into that, but I'm not sure how convincing I'd be right now. This is getting too comfortable to be wise, but I want one more night with him. I'm not ready to let go again. I'm hiding from things I should be dealing with, but he makes it so damn easy to turn away from reality.

Karaoke is in full swing when we walk into Jolene's. We're almost done with our second glasses when the first notes of Islands in the Stream play. I'm instantly infuriated that someone else has the nerve to do our song, and just as quickly it dawns on me how ridiculous that is.

Bryce laughs. "I got pissed, too. It's okay."

"Could you feel my anger?"

"Your whole body tensed."

"Old habits." I don't tell him that as soon as the anger faded, the desire to take the stage and show those conformists how it's done took over. They are staying true to the original lyrics, of course. The melody is another story. They're wine drunk and tone deaf, and they're making me want a third glass.

I already had a few at Katie's. I should stop, but I really want one more glass. Bryce notices me surveying my last ounce. "One more?"

"Sure. Why not?"

By the end of my third glass, that niggling agitation won't go away. I mean, they ruined the song. If you're not going to parody it, at least give it the respect it deserves. They basically made a mockery of it. At least our changes are entertaining. Crowd pleasers.

Bryce eyes me suspiciously. "I can see the wheels turning in that pretty head of yours. What's going on in there?"

"They did a terrible job on our song."

"The worst I've ever heard."

"At least you and I can actually sing."

"We're pretty good together."

"It would almost be a shame to let these people leave with the memory of the massacre that took place on that stage."

"We could wipe that performance from their minds for good."

"It's almost like we have a responsibility to the community."

"Practically our civil duty."

We clink glasses. "To our version," I say.

"To the stage." He pulls me by my hand through the tables. I think we may have cut in line, but really our performance can't wait. They'll see.

When we reach our grand finale, and I yank up my shirt for his eyes only, I suddenly see what I hadn't seen before. They've added tables to the side of the stage. And I just showed my boobs to about a dozen strangers. Bryce is dying laughing. I cover myself quickly and pull him off stage.

We make our way back through the tables, getting a few high fives and a few more disapproving looks. You can't please all the people.

"Close out our tab, and get me out of here."

"I closed it after my last trip to the bar. Keep walking."

Our laughter sounds so much louder as we walk out into the cool night air. Neither one of us can stop. Damn, I hope this is still funny tomorrow.

"What's that?" I ask, pointing to a patch of grass at the edge of the lot. I sprint for it and hold it up to the skies, shaking it above my head. "It's not neon green, but it's not empty either."

"It's like fate."

"The guardian angel of graffiti artists has thrown this down for us. It would be sacrilege to disregard her blessing."

"Or it fell out of someone's bag while they were leaving the hardware store."

"Oh, don't try to get logical on me now."

"You're right. It was clearly sent from above."

I walk toward the wall, shaking the can. The moment the stream of black paint hits the bricks, I'm inspired. Standing on the bumper of a stranger's car, I stretch to put the crowning tip on my masterpiece. The moment I close the gap between the head and the shaft, the flash of red and blue lights causes me to lose my balance and fall behind the car.

Tossing the can to the side, I push myself up and wipe grass off my jeans. Bryce's eyes are huge. "Shh," I say. "Be cool. Nobody's touching a can of paint. They can't prove shit."

The officer steps out of the patrol car, and I laugh. "Hey, Mikey."

"Fuck me," he says. "I should've known."

"What are you doing here?" I ask, sauntering over to Bryce as if there's nothing to see on the wall.

"I'm responding to a call about an act of lewd and lascivious behavior, specifically, public nudity, but wait, there's more! You also walked your bar tab? What the hell, man?"

"That's bullshit," Bryce says. "I closed out my tab."

"I'll go in and talk to the manager. In the meantime, the two of you can be my guests." He opens the back door of the patrol car.

"You can't be serious," I say. "What are you going to do if I run? Because I'm pretty sure you can't catch me."

"Peri, I'm begging you. Please don't complicate this. Just wait in the car with Bryce until I can sort through this."

Bryce climbs into the car, still laughing. No way. I'm not getting in the backseat of a cop car. This is ridiculous.

Mike looks up at the wall. "Oh, for fuck's sake! Come on, Peri. Why?"

"I don't know what you're talking about."

"I am trying so hard not to have to arrest you."

"For what? My tits are not a crime."

"I'm sure they're still as beautiful as ever, but I've—"

"You don't fucking comment on her body, Maltsberger!" Bryce is climbing back out of the cop car.

Aw, hell, this is about to escalate. "Hey, it's no big deal. We're cool. Let's just wait in the backseat, okay?" I put my hands on Bryce's chest and try to push him back toward the car. His nostrils are already flared and his arms are flexed. "Are you really going to refuse to climb into a backseat with me?"

He smiles, but he doesn't relax any.

"Let's just hang out in the car while he goes in and confirms the tab was paid."

Bryce acquiesces, and we climb into the backseat together. Mike comes over to close the door. "Please keep your shirt on, Peri. Y'all just behave for a few more minutes, okay? I can only disregard so much."

"We'll be good."

Mike goes inside Jolene's, and Bryce and I laugh far harder than we have a right to, given our circumstances. He comes back out and opens the door on Bryce's side. "All right. There was a miscommunication about the tab. That's all cleared up now."

"Great," Bryce and I say at the same time. We slide toward the door, but Mike shakes his head.

"However, your performance is still a problem. Customers complained. A topless woman isn't against the law unless she disrupts the peace. Apparently, y'all were disruptive. Not to mention, the crooked penis now overlooking their parking lot. I've got to take y'all in."

"Crooked?" I roll my eyes. "You wish you had that curve."

Bryce's head falls back, but he's not laughing. "Fine, Mike. Flex your fucking badge. Let's just get this shit over with."

"Sorry, man. Seat belts, please."

We buckle up, and Mike closes the door.

"This is outrageous." I say. "I can't believe we're going to jail for being the best singers in the bar."

Mike laughs as he slides behind the wheel, but pretends like he's not listening.

It hits me like a ton of bricks that I have no one to call. No one. That's a sobering thought. Literally. "Who can we call?"

"My first choice would be Keller, but he's in a house full of sound asleep little boys and a newborn baby."

"Lisa?"

"Oh, hell no. I am not calling my sister. I'd never hear the end of it."

"We're going to have to call Katie with a K, aren't we?"

"I can't think of anyone else right now."

I cringe. "When we get to the station, we can flip a coin. Heads, you call her. Tails, you call her."

Bryce laughs at that, rich, robust laughter like we're still back at Katie's house, sharing old stories. But this is a whole new story, and I'd give anything if we didn't have to share it with another living soul. Ever.

He wouldn't be in the back of a police car right now if I weren't here. If I were in Houston, there's not a snowball's chance in hell I'd be in one. Maybe we really are bad for each other.

There was nothing in the grief books about getting arrested for flashing your boobs in a wine bar, or spray-painting dicks on historic buildings.

Some people might say those things fall under the chapters on uncharacteristic behavior, but those people have no idea how utterly characteristic it is for me. The old me, who apparently can't keep her ass in that little box in the back of my memory where she's supposed to live now. I guess that makes her the current me.

Only in this town. And with this boy. Man. Whatever.

"I told you if I got arrested while I was in town, I wanted it to be for something better than a graffitied dick."

"To be fair, we're not here just because of the graffiti." He takes my hand. "But if it'll make you feel better, I think you could definitely land a swing on Maltsberger."

23

Bryce

Katie's eyes are ablaze when we're released. "This is what y'all get for going to Jolene's without me."

"Guess I probably won't be getting invited to any more dinner parties at your place," I say.

She gives me a look that could kill as we walk out of the station. It's a shame she doesn't want to have kids because that's a scary mom look if I've ever seen one.

"Don't try to be cute right now, Bryce." She turns to Peri, takes a deep breath, and asks if she's okay.

"I have no idea," Peri says. "Actually, I think I might not be okay at all."

What the hell does she mean by that? "You're fine," I say in what I think is a calm, reassuring voice.

"Fine? You think I'm fine, Bryce? I'm twenty-nine-years-old and just caught a vandalism charge! And there's no guarantee Jolene's will drop the public indecency charges against us, no matter what Mikey *thinks* will happen. There is nothing even remotely okay about any of this."

"Where am I taking everybody?" Katie asks once we're in her car.

"Take us back to my truck at Jolene's."

She looks at Peri, waiting for her to agree before she puts the car in drive. I hold my breath in the backseat, staring at her profile and hoping like hell she'll say that's what she wants, too.

"Yeah," she finally says with a nod. "There's no need for you to have drop us at separate places."

"You got it."

At least Katie still thinks I have a shot. She wouldn't have even asked that question if she didn't. I'd be dropped off, and she'd be driving away with Peri before I could even wave goodbye.

I guess I should feel as bad about us getting arrested as Peri does, but it's funny to me. And it felt good, to be honest. Like old times. The world's not going to end because we had a spontaneous moment. We didn't hurt anybody.

If we were back together again, it's not like we'd get into trouble on a regular basis the way we did back then, but tonight was fun, dammit. She needed to blow off steam, and I needed to be the one she did it with.

When we get back to my truck, Katie looks at the dick on the side of Crawford's and bursts out laughing. "You forgot to sign it."

"I'm not signing my *dicks on bricks* collection these days." Peri shakes her head at her latest creation.

"Anybody who knows you would've known it was yours, anyway." Katie laughs again.

"Good to know I have a recognizable style."

From the backseat, I can see the curve of Peri's smile start to form as Katie teases her. She was so close to the CKaties. I don't know who her best friends are these days, or if she shares things like this with them, but I know spending time with her oldest friends has been good for her. I'm good for her, too. And I'm going to make her see that. I just need a little more time.

I slide out of the car and lean in to hug Katie through the window. "Thanks again. Tell Derek I'm sorry for the late-night call."

"Derek's fine. He just shook his head and asked if he should come with me. I told him to go back to sleep. Try not to get my friend into any more trouble tonight."

"No promises." I shrug and raise my eyebrows.

"Get out of my car, Bryce Callaway." We laugh, but as I'm pulling my head back, she whispers, "Talk her into staying longer."

"I'm going to give it my best shot."

Peri is waiting for me by the truck, still staring at the graffiti. She's tilting her head from one side to the other.

"I guess it's true then," I say. "Every artist is a critic?"

"My work actually sells in galleries. Not a lot, but I'm not painting a lot right now either. If anyone who owns my work knew I did this, they'd probably burn their piece."

"Well, if it's any consolation, I'll model for you anytime."

"Surprisingly, dicks aren't my usual subject these days."

We get in the truck, and she's laughing, which has to be a good sign. "What do you mostly paint now?"

"I did an urban decay series a few years ago that sold really well, and I add to it from time to time."

"Urban, huh? I guess I wouldn't be a very good model for that."

"I think you could live anywhere and do just fine."

"With you, I could."

"Don't, Bryce."

"Okay. Let's get you home." My stomach twists itself in knots as I back out and wait for her to say she doesn't want me to stay.

"Can we go to your place? I don't want to go back to mine after everything that happened tonight." She picks at her fingernails in her lap. "I know how stupid that sounds. Neither one of my parents is going to be there, but I just don't want to walk into their house feeling like a disappointment again. Not tonight."

"Hey, look at me, Pear." She lifts her eyes a few inches. "Tonight got a little crazy, but when the sun comes up tomorrow, it's not going to matter. It was a blip, that's all. Done in the blink of an eye. It's already in the past."

"The past always catches up to you, though."

"Sometimes even the good parts." I smile at her.

"Yeah. Even the good parts."

Her smile is sad, and I don't know if it's grief sad or because of me sad. "I'd love to see your recent paintings. You got pictures?"

"Yeah." Her smile brightens. "I'll show them to you when we get to the house."

Crash barrels past us as soon as I open the door. "He always acts like he hasn't been let out in days. I swear he went out right before I left for Katie's."

"He gets excited. He can't help it."

"You'd take up for him if he ate a hole in the wall."

"He gets hungry. He can't help it."

"Exactly." I laugh and turn on the lights in the living room. "You want some water?"

"I definitely need some water. Why does jail make you so thirsty?"

"You were in jail for less than thirty minutes. Red wine makes you thirsty."

"Oh, yeah. I guess it could've been that."

She's looking at the pictures on the piano when I come back. "Lisa's kids are so grown."

"If you ask them, they are. Lisa thinks my nephew acts like me."

"That's a harsh accusation." She sips from the water, and the faint traces of lipstick she's still wearing leave a print on the rim of the glass. "You still play?" Her fingers slide silently over the keys.

"Sometimes." Crash headbutts the door. When I let him in, he runs right for the couch and claims the middle cushion. "No way, bud. She has to sit next to me so she can show me her paintings." As if he understands everything I've said, he lifts up and clomps over a few feet before collapsing back down.

Peri takes the spot he's just vacated so she can pet him. I sit on the other end of the couch. "All right, let's see this urban decay."

She scrolls through pictures on her phone, and I try not to stare at the passing images. Faces jump out at me, though. All unfamiliar. Not all female. I know she's not seeing anyone back in Houston, though. Nothing serious, anyway. I've spent too much time with her for there to have been no awkward texts or calls.

"Okay, this is the first one I sold." Her screen shows a painting of a crumbling tan brick building with a flowering vine growing through the cracked mortar. There's a bright blue butterfly hovering over a cluster of tiny yellow flowers. A weird scene of angels flying over old cars takes up the other side of the painting. It's some sort of parade, I think. She painted from the center of a fading mural out to the edge of the broken bricks. The wall is nearly collapsed on the end, but looks like it's still standing complete in the section with the mural, as if the art is holding it together in the middle, like time can't destroy it there.

"It's art within art. You painted someone else's painting."

"A portion of it. The point is that it's still cool and interesting, even though the canvas it's painted on is falling apart. It's not vibrant and new anymore, but it still makes you stop and think when you look at it. But without it, no one would look at that building. Sometimes, there's something beautiful there, even without a mural or graffiti.

"That building served a purpose at one point, maybe a lot of different purposes over time, but now, it's not useful in a way that anyone can charge rent for, so people just see a useless eyesore, something that needs to be torn down. They don't even stop to appreciate the history or the art someone created on it before they bring in the wrecking ball."

"Are you on a committee to save old murals on old buildings?" It seems like exactly the kind of thing she'd be involved in.

"No, but if anyone ever asked me to join one, I might."

"You *might*? You know who you're talking to, right? You would at the very least sign a petition."

"I'd definitely sign a petition." She scrolls to the next photo. No mural on this one, but a fallen bird's nest and cherry tomatoes ripening on a bush that looks like it's growing out of a pile of red bricks. There are no trees around for the nest to have fallen from. Maybe it fell somewhere else and was blown there.

"I wonder who planted those tomatoes."

"Maybe birds planted them," she says with a little defensiveness in her voice, like she's defending the birds' abilities.

"They could have. They eat the tomatoes from somebody's garden, fly to an abandoned lot with a decaying building and shit the seeds there. It makes as much sense as anything."

"I saw people who were living under the bridge across the street pick those tomatoes. That could've been the only thing they ate that day. And now, the building is gone and so are the tomatoes. Nobody cared that people might've needed them. Because mostly, we don't care about each other."

"That's not true here."

"It's true everywhere, Bryce. It's just not true for you. You have people. Not everyone does."

"Sometimes, I used to wonder if you were the most cynical person I knew, or the one with the biggest heart of all."

"Maybe I just have a great big cynical heart."

"No, you don't."

Her next painting is a broken bottle of orange soda that's spilled into the cracks in an asphalt parking lot. A hummingbird is drinking from it. There are waves of refraction rising from the surface of the asphalt beyond the edges of the soda-filled cracks. You can almost feel the heat when you look at it.

"Did you paint that from a photo?"

"From memory. I saw it, but I could've never gotten a good picture of it."

"So you created one."

"Yep. The guy who bought it is apparently a big deal with the Houston Symphony. He said it had a musical quality to it. I have no idea what he meant by that, but the gallery manager said he went on and on about it. I guess it's the heat waves."

"No, I think it's something else. It's in all your paintings."

"If you say so. I am definitely not a musician."

"And I've never been a painter, but your work creates a mood, the way music does, but you do it visually."

She looks up into my eyes, and I want to say more, tell her that we're still alike in more ways than we'll ever be different. I wish I was the kind of guy who could say some sappy shit about the intersection of music and painting, and make it meaningful, but I don't know how to put stuff like that into words. So, I kiss her instead.

Her mouth melds with mine, but the eagerness in her kiss and the tension in her body feel like the first night we were together here, like she's chasing something, or trying to outrun it. "Slow down. Let's take our time tonight."

That soft smile she's showing now makes me weak. It always did. Anytime she let her guard down and went soft, she owned me. When she's hot and hungry, we own each other, but when she's vulnerable with me, I want to be her safety net, her home. It's what I've always wanted with her. Beyond all the recklessness, the pranks, the stubborn battles we had . . . I loved her in the boring moments in between even more than I loved the dares and the adrenaline rushes.

She was everybody's favorite girl when she was wild, so that's how they remember her. Most people never got to see her like this, and I'll never be able to forget it.

I lead her to my room and take my time undressing her, kissing her neck and her shoulders after I take off her sweater. Her fingers work their way down the buttons of my shirt. When I remove it, her hands roam over my chest and my arms. Pulling her into me, I rub her back and enjoy the feeling of her skin against mine.

Once we're fully undressed, I fold the covers back so she can climb into my bed, where she belongs. I follow her between the sheets and press my forehead to hers. "It might be true that we wouldn't have made it if we'd stayed together back then, but it's no less true that you are still everything I have ever wanted." I kiss her again to save us both from the pain of her response. She might've tried to explain why we still wouldn't work or how we don't know each other anymore, and I don't want to hear any of that. The way she's kissing me tells me she didn't want to say any of it either.

My thumb brushes over her nipple, and it pebbles under my touch. She inhales sharply and steals my breath, tempting me to devour her, but I resist. I still want to take my time with her tonight. Breaking the kiss, I stare down at her breast, watch my hand cup and squeeze. Warmth and softness fill my palm, and I close my eyes for a moment to enjoy the perfection.

Letting my hand drift lower, I watch as it dips down to trace her waist and back up and over her hip. She's lost some definition since she's been back in Copper. Seeing her toned abs and legs that night in my kitchen when she dropped her jumpsuit about made me cream my jeans, but this softer body is sexy as hell, too.

She'll go back to Houston and get back to her workout routine, all her routines that transform her into the woman she wants to be, but right now, she's softer in every way, and I want to freeze time.

Her eyes are mapping me, too. My hand slips between her legs, and I massage her inner thigh. She rolls onto her back and spreads them to make it easier. I smile at the beauty of her lying next to me so defenseless. So mine.

I can't resist sliding my hand up to her pussy, slipping a finger inside. Her moan when I do it is needy and sweet. Taking my finger from her pussy and trailing it around her nipple, I lick my lips at the way her skin glistens with her arousal coating it, and then I suck it off with my finger back inside her.

The way her fingers slide into my hair and her back arches is as familiar as it ever was. My teeth gently graze her nipple and she squirms. I insert another finger, and her pussy clenches immediately. Using the heel of my hand, I rub firm circles over her clit. She doesn't scream when she comes, but her fingernails scrape against my scalp, and her pussy creams around my fingers. Her walls contract again as an aftershock rolls through her core. I groan at the sensation of her body trying to recover.

She loves to be fucked immediately after she comes, and I want her to love every second of this, but I want to keep looking at her, watching her enjoying herself. I pull her onto me, and she assumes a wide straddle, rising up to position my dick where she needs it.

Her eyes are glazed and her body is loose, but when she slides her tight pussy down my cock, the sheer bliss of it causes every muscle in my body to contract for a few seconds. We both moan, and there is nothing as good as sharing her pleasure and having her share mine when a moment hits us both the same.

The sight of her stretching around me as she continues to bury my dick in her heat is making it hard not to buck my hips and fuck it the rest of the way inside her, but I want her to be in control for a while. When she's fully seated, another moan escapes me. She lifts back off just as slowly, and I can't help but tilt up a little.

She smiles and picks up her pace, rolling her hips at the bottom to grind against me each time she comes down.

My hands go to her hips, but I'm careful not to guide her, not yet, anyway. I'm still holding out on myself so she can do what she likes, but my fingers dig into her perfect little ass when she grinds on me again.

Without warning, she lifts up and turns around. Reverse cowgirl has never been my favorite because it takes a woman's tits out of view, but Peri's hair hangs down her back, begging me to wrap it around my fist, and I do like the way that looks. I pull a little and she whimpers, but it's for show. And I'm perfectly okay with her making hot sounds just for my benefit. If she's trying to manipulate me, it's working.

But when my hips jerk and my dick lurches inside her, her pussy gets wetter. I'm having an effect on her, too. She's watching herself in the mirror over my dresser. God, she looks beautiful riding my dick. Seeing the reflections of her tits is cruel, though—the epitome of being able to look but not touch.

She pinches her own nipples when she realizes I'm watching her in the mirror as well. There's no keeping my hips still now. I have to switch this up before she makes me come.

I lift her off me. "Get on your hands and knees."

She attempts face down, ass up, but I pull her up onto all fours. "No, I need to be able to reach your clit."

My hand reaches around to play with her clit while my dick sinks back into her pussy. Hopefully, I can get her there quick because I'm not going to last long. Her first round of spasms goes off and my dick swells. I take a breath and hold it, trying to maintain everywhere—no change in the speed or pressure I'm rubbing her clit with, no more thrusting into her, just focusing on getting her off. She's so close. The clenching tightens and her breath quickens. *There we go. Let go, baby. Let go.*

Seconds after her orgasm crests, mine rolls through my body like a tsunami. I've got no self-control left when she comes on my dick.

I hold her when she gets back from the bathroom, still trying to steady my breathing. There was no pain, no praise, no degradation, no daddy, just plain old sex, and it was still fucking fantastic. "We're still good at the vanilla stuff, too."

She laughs. "Your idea of vanilla might not line up with some people's."

"What? I didn't spank you or hold you down or call you dirty names. You didn't call me any names. That was some vanilla shit, but it was good."

"I actually think when some people say vanilla, they mean straight missionary, no change in positions, no sucking body fluids off one another, no touching themselves in the mirror, no—"

"That's not even vanilla. That's unflavored."

"It's some people's version of vanilla."

"Well, I feel sorry for those people."

"Me, too."

She snuggles her head into the crook of my shoulder.

"Sweet dreams, criminal."

"Sweet dreams, accomplice."

I blow strands of her hair away from my mouth and hold her while she falls asleep.

24

Peri

I TURN MY PHONE to show Katie the option that I think is her on the online payment system. "Just confirm this is your account so I can send you the money."

"No way. Bailing you and Bryce out of jail was fun for me. Besides, I like having you owe me."

"But I don't like owing anybody anything."

"I know. That actually makes it even better for me."

"What could you possibly blackmail me with? I'm an open book."

"I'll just use it to guilt you into things."

"Like what?"

"Like staying in town another couple weeks."

I set my phone on my kitchen counter. "I've got roofers coming this afternoon to give me estimates."

"How'd you get three roofing companies to come out on a Saturday?"

"I'm very persuasive."

I pick up a box and head for the front door. "Can you get this for me?"

Katie holds the door open, and then she follows me out to my car. "What's in the boxes?"

"Mom's clothes for the thrift shop."

"Aw, Peri. You didn't have to box that stuff up alone. I meant it when I said I'd help."

"I know, but I wanted to do it alone."

She nods and makes the next few trips with me to help load the rest.

We hug goodbye at my car. Her stare goes right through me. She knows. Or she suspects, anyway.

I've scheduled the roofers half an hour apart, but the first two show up at the same time. The third is thirty minutes late, but he makes it, and I'm glad. I don't know what it is, but I just like him better than the others. He seems trustworthy and more competent. Not like I know anything about roofing, but I know a little about pitching yourself to a customer, and he's the best of the three in that regard.

Katie slows in front of my house, rolls down her window, and waves. "Hey, I've got a showing around the corner. You want to do happy hour when I'm done?"

"I'm not drinking tonight."

"They have appetizers at happy hour, too."

"Not tonight."

Her smile falls. I know she doesn't have a showing around the corner. It's obvious she was driving by to see if my car was still here. Katie can't do subtle. "All right. Well, I'll text you later to see if you changed your mind."

"Okay." There's no point in telling her not to.

The last roofing contractor drives away, and Katie follows him down the street. I doublecheck that I locked the front door before I head to the thrift shop. My eyes close, and I let my hand rest on the knob. The volume of my heartbeat increases until it's all I can hear.

A boy that looks like he's probably still in high school helps me unload the boxes at the thrift shop. He's cute. I bet he plays football, thinks his current girlfriend is the one, makes all his buddies laugh, and let's his dog sleep in his bed.

"Do you need a receipt for your taxes, ma'am?"

Ma'am? Ouch. "No, I'm good. Thanks for the help."

I spot two more high school boys on Main Street, scrubbing away my last artistic contribution to Crawford's. They're laughing as they do it, and that makes me smile. A trio of teenage girls walks out of the donut shop and runs across the street to see what the boys are washing off. Copper kids . . . I bet they're all going to be okay, no matter where they end up. Maybe in a dozen years or so, they'll get together and share a laugh about that time some drunk woman painted a crooked dick on the side of the hardware store. I hope they do.

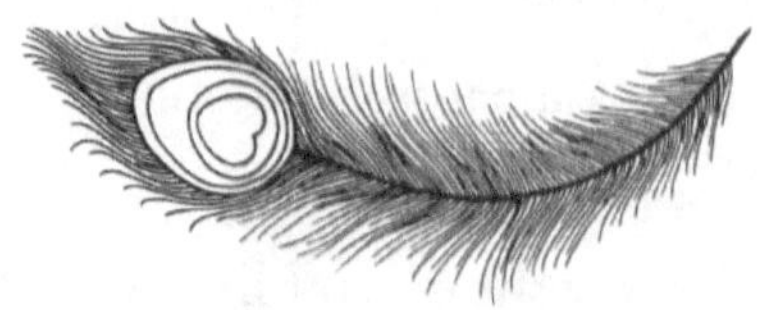

Traffic is at a standstill on the Loop. I've been staring at the sign for my exit for twenty minutes. It's less than a mile ahead, but we haven't moved an inch. I'm stuck. My eyes burn and my shoulders and neck ache. I just want to get home, fall into my bed, and not get out of it again until Monday.

Finally, the cars in front of me crawl forward. I feel like I'm literally crawling on my hands and knees to reach the damn exit ramp. Loud music and Buc-ee's coffee can only keep me upright behind the wheel for so long.

One more red light, one left turn, and then it's over.

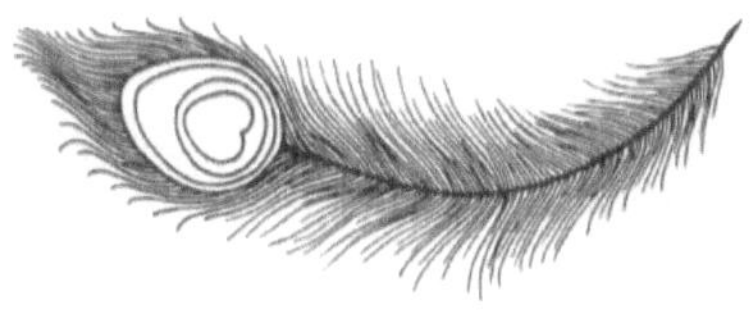

My apartment is freezing. I forgot to tell the woman I was paying to water my plants to turn off the air conditioner. Why didn't she ask? She must've frozen her ass off in here that last few times. It was so hot the day I left, and now it's cold enough for a coat in Houston.

The central heat kicks on with that stale burning smell it always makes when you turn it on for the first time of the season.

I kick off my shoes, but my complete exhaustion has been reduced to nothing more than an irritable tiredness, probably from the arctic blast when I walked through my door. There's no way I can sleep yet, so I curl up on the couch with a blanket and point the remote at the TV.

People move and speak on the screen but I can't hear what they're saying. The voices in my head are too loud, screaming doubts and questions and accusations. Leaving was the right choice, the only choice. I hear my mom's reaffirming voice. *The easy choice and the right one are rarely the same.*

Never, Mama. Never are they the same when it comes to him.

25

Bryce

I KICK AT THE shrub cuttings piled around my feet. These holly bushes have needed to be cut back for weeks. I've had my head up my ass, acting like shit just takes care of itself. Keller's tires come hauling ass up my drive, kicking up dust. He's shaking his head at me through the windshield. What the hell's on his mind?

He hops out and whistles. "Crash!"

My dog stops digging at the fence line and comes running at full-speed, not falling once, but I can't even take a moment to be proud of him because Keller's holding his door open like he's about to . . . there's no way he's about to—.

"Load up!"

Crash obeys that command like I gave it to him. "Where the hell do you think you're going with my dog?"

He slams the door, trapping my dog in his truck, though from the look on Crash's face he's all too happy to be in there.

"He's coming to hang out with my kids for a few days while you go to Houston."

I hack off another section of holly. "We both know that'd be nothing but a waste of gas."

"Get your ass in your fucking truck and go shoot your fucking shot!" With his hand on his truck door, he gives me a one-shoulder shrug. "Because the way I see it, you could burn a tank of gas tonight, or you could wait around and see if maybe she shows back up in another ten or twelve years. I guess do whichever one makes the most sense to you." With that weak-ass challenge thrown, he gets in his truck and leaves.

He just took my fucking dog.

Lisa's car turns through the gate. *Great. She's just what I fucking need right now.*

"Where's Keller taking Crash?"

"He's having a play date with Keller's boys."

"Oh, okay. Does he do that often?"

"What do you want, Lisa?"

"Geez. Who pissed on your parade?" She holds out a curling iron. "I told Peri she could have this but she hasn't come by the salon to get it. I tried to take it to her, but she wasn't home. I didn't want to leave it outside. Are you going to see her later?"

I stare at the silver barrel gleaming in the sun for a few beats before I reach for it. "Yeah. Yeah, I'm going to see her in about four and a half hours."

"That was specific. You could've just said tonight." She looks around at my landscaping handiwork. "What did these holly bushes ever do to you?"

"Go home, Lisa."

"Damn, you're extra grumpy today. Tell Peri I said hi."

"Will do."

My grip tightens on the pink-handled curling iron clutched in one hand while the pruning shears fall from my other. Half-functioning on all fronts. I see what Lisa saw now: I've definitely butchered these shrubs. The last thing I need to do is go to Houston.

What would I even do, anyway, just show up and say, "Hi, my sister asked me to give this to you?"

Katie with a K would probably mail this thing to her if I asked her to.

I could throw it away. Toss it on the ground and run over with my truck. Donate it to the thrift shop. I'm sure she can afford to buy one there.

Nothing clears my head like a nice, long drive, though. I text Katie to get Peri's address, tell her I need to mail something to her. If I'm doing this, I don't want her to have any advanced warning. I want her unguarded gut reaction—her mumbling-over-chickens-moment-of-shock. It's only fair.

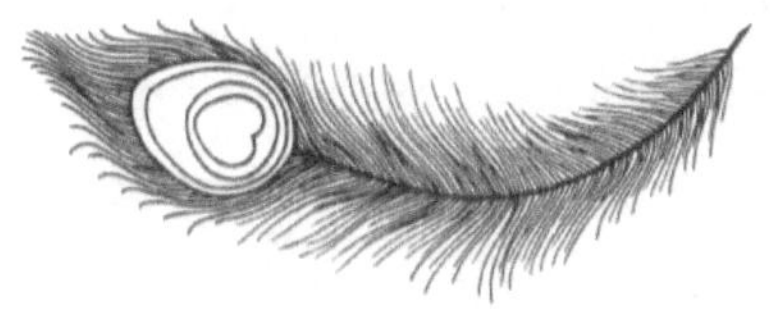

How are this many people on the fucking road at eleven o'clock on a Tuesday night? The light turns green for the third time since I've been sitting in line waiting on it. I finally make it through, and take the first left turn. I see the apartment building on the block ahead. My eyes burn and I'm still not sure what the hell I'm going to say to her, or if I can even get inside.

Worst case, I guess I'll text her from the street and hope she doesn't tell me to go home. Fuck, this could all go so damn wrong.

I make the block in search of an open spot. The parking garage is closed off by an automatic door. Even if I followed another car in, I remember she said I'd need an access card to get on the elevator. From the way she described it, this place is a fortress.

My alarm beeps when I click the fob over my shoulder as I walk away from my truck. Now or never.

Shit. The curling iron.

I backtrack to get my excuse for being here. Like it matters. The cord comes unwound and tangles around my hand. I stop on the sidewalk and take my time rewrapping it. When I look up, a couple is heading for the front door of the building.

I sprint to catch up to them, but make sure I hang back enough that they won't expect me to pull out an access card. They smile and say hi like they think I belong here. This is a good sign. I follow them onto the elevator, but unless they're going to the fifth floor I'm going to be stuck.

What the hell am I going to do? Just keeping following random people onto the elevator from every floor until somebody finally goes to the fifth? This is the stupidest damn thing I've ever done.

The guy reaches for the control panel and presses . . . the number five button. Well, what do you fucking know? I guess somebody's looking out for me.

I hang back again when we leave the elevator so they don't realize I have no idea which direction I'm supposed to go. They seem eager to get where they're going, not at all concerned about me.

Of course, I choose the wrong direction. I tell myself that's a good thing because the couple from the elevator is already inside their apartment now. They won't see me looking at numbers like I'm lost.

There it is: Unit 511B.

She's on the other side of that door. Or she's out having a great night, dancing away all the shit she went through back in Copper. Only one way to find out.

I knock on the door before I realize there are voices beyond it. She's got company. This surprise visit is going to be more awkward than I bargained for.

Peri opens the door already looking like she's seen a ghost. It's clear she's looked through the peep hole. She knew exactly who she was going to find in the hallway. "Bryce, what the hell are you doing here? How'd you even get in?"

The guy from the elevator answers for me. "Um, we let him in."

"Y'all know each other?"

"No," the woman says. "But he seemed like he belonged here, like he knew where he was going."

"You okay, Peri?" the man asks, squaring his shoulders like he's preparing to escort me out of the building if she tells him she doesn't want me here. At least she has good neighbors. Who show up at her house at eleven on a Sunday night. Weird, but okay.

"Yeah," she says. "It's fine. I'm just in shock."

I extend the curling iron. "Lisa asked me to give this to you."

"You drove all the way to Houston to bring me a curling iron?"

"What do you think?"

The woman steps toward the door. "Well, we just wanted to see you and make sure you were okay."

"If you need anything, we're right next door," the guy says, eyeing me less warily, but definitely committing my face to memory.

"Thanks for the fix." Peri holds up a to-go container.

They hug her on the way out, and I step out of the way so they can go to their own apartment. She doesn't invite me in, just stands there, staring at me.

"You knew if you showed up this late, I wouldn't turn you away."

"No, I still don't know that. You could tell me to fuck right off into the sun at any moment."

She opens the door wide. "Come in."

I step inside. "For what it's worth, I didn't plan to show up this late. Or at all."

"So, you accidentally drove four and a half hours?"

"I love you. It's still you for me. It's always been you, Peri. If you don't love me, I need you to say it plainly. Don't say you care about me or that part of you will always love me. That's not what I'm asking. I want to know if you love me like I love you, because nothing less than that would give us a fighting chance at this point." I run my hand through my hair. "That's all I've got. I don't have a long, impassioned speech, no list of well-thought-out ways we can make this work. All I know is I love you through and through. I fucking love you."

She blinks away tears. "And if I say I don't love you like that, how long do you think you'll keep loving me that way?"

"Forever, Pear. Forever. I've tried to not love you. It's never going to happen."

"But how, Bryce?" Tears stream down her cheeks. "How are we supposed to do this?"

"I don't know if we are. Talk to me."

"I fucking love you so much it makes my stomach hurt. Every goddamn day."

"Every goddamn day, huh?"

"Yes. And it's your fault." She laughs through the tears. "You really think we stand a fighting chance of figuring this out?"

"Oh, I don't think I've ever known anybody as good at fighting as we are." I step toward her, grab her waist and pull her into me. "So, you ready to get really good at sexting?"

She sniffles. "What makes you think I'm not already an expert?"

"I can't wait to see your skills in action. But you can go ahead and turn your phone off for tonight."

"Can I eat this first?" She holds the to-go box up next to my head.

"I'm trying really hard not to be offended right now. Whatever is in that box better be the stuff of food fantasies."

"It's the world's best strawberry cake."

"The world's best? Am I supposed to just take your word for that?" I flip the box open.

She scoops a bite onto two fingers and brings it to my mouth. I swallow the cake and suck her fingers clean. "Not bad." I run my finger through the fluffy frosting and tease it across her bottom lip. "For a first course."

26

Peri

I'M STILL ON PERSONAL leave from my job, but Bryce has to make early morning calls to be sure his guys can handle the shop for a few days. He says he'll probably have to take some calls and maybe make a few more before the day's over.

I never expected him to be here at all; I sure don't expect him to ignore his business while I show him around, starting with breakfast at Bosscat, because there's no way Bryce in Houston traffic while hangry is a good idea. I'm not trying to sell him on the city, just want him to see where I live, how I live.

He spins his coffee cup on the table. "I want to talk about it," he says, and I know exactly which *it* he means.

"We really don't have to," I say. "I forgave you for that a long time ago, Bryce. We were kids. It was just another prank."

"No, it wasn't, and you know it. I was mad at you. I had no idea what all it would lead to, but I didn't turn your name in as a joke. I was hurt and pissed off, so I wanted to fuck up your world a little. I thought you were fucking up mine, and I retaliated. It was immature and careless, but I genuinely had no idea you'd be investigated so thoroughly, or lose that scholarship."

"I know. The moment I said I thought we should break up before we went off to separate schools, I could see the resentment in your eyes. There was no reasoning with you."

"None. I wish somebody could've knocked some sense into me before I picked up that fucking phone."

"I won't lie. The investigation sucked, Bryce. All the speculation that followed sucked worse. But things worked out. I ended up transferring into the University of Houston my sophomore year, and it was a better fit than my first choice would've ever been. This city overall was such a good fit for me. Good things have happened for me here."

"You could never be happy back in Copper. And I'm not sure I could be happy here, Pear."

"You didn't let me finish. I've loved living here, but I've been feeling antsy for a while now. I'm not saying I want to move right away, but if things worked out for us, I'd be open to living somewhere else. Nowhere as small as Copper, but it doesn't have to be somewhere as big as Houston either. But what would you do about your shop?"

"Open a new one wherever we ended up. Start over. Or go to work for somebody else. Maybe go back to commercial design. I keep my license active."

"Shit. I forget you're actually an architect."

"I still do some contract stuff, enough to keep my skills current. I could get a job."

"You had one. With a big firm in Dallas. I heard things through the grapevine for a while. How'd you give that up and move back to Copper?"

"Dad was gone and Mom was sick. I couldn't leave Lisa to handle it all. It wouldn't have been fair. I never planned to stay in Copper. Leaving isn't out of the question."

"So . . . what you're saying is, if I decide I can put up with you long-term, we can probably figure it out?" God, he looks gorgeous, smiling at me with the steam from his coffee still rising between his hands. He's overdue for a haircut and tired, but he looks happy. For the first time in months, I feel like it's okay to be happy. And I am.

"What I'm saying is, I'm not letting you go again, so we *will* figure it out."

"Stop. You're making my stomach hurt."

"I love you, too." He takes a sip of his coffee, and I watch him, wondering how we could be us again after all these years, but here we are. "Your apartment building is not as secure as you think it is, by the way."

"Can you ever just let a nice moment be?"

"I don't want you walking around with a false sense of security, that's all. It was way too damn easy for me to get on that elevator."

"Right. I'm sure you looked like such a threat, with your pink curling iron."

"I'm just saying—"

"And I'm just asking you to stop."

He stares at me, and I can practically hear all the unspoken warnings and safety advice begging to escape his lips. "You're going to drive me crazy for the rest of my life, aren't you?"

"If you're lucky."

"I gotta be honest, I'm feeling pretty damn lucky right now."

A call lights up my phone screen. "It's Katie with a K."

"Yeah, you might want to let her go to voicemail for a few days, give her some time to cool off. The other one, too."

"You think they'll forgive me?"

"You are surprisingly hard to stay mad at."

"Yeah, for you, but that's just because I'm so good at sucking your dick and calling you Daddy."

Holy shit! When that did that waiter get here? What the hell, is he part panther?

I drop my head and sigh.

Bryce's laughter from across the table spawns a reel of happy memories, and a truckload of hope for a couple reckless kids who might finally be ready to love each other.

27

Bryce

18 months later . . .

I ROUND THE CORNER into our new kitchen and set the bags of chips Peri sent me out for onto the counter. She glances over her shoulder to make sure I got the right kind.

"Bryce Callaway, after all these years, you finally bought me roses?"

"They didn't have any red ones."

"It's okay. I like yellow better." She blows me a kiss, and then goes back to unwrapping new wine glasses and hanging them in the cabinet I custom built for her collection. "Do me a favor and get a vase down from the storage closet in the hall?"

I'm sure I chose the wrong one, but it's a vase. I add water and drop the roses in, knowing she'll probably take them back out and rearrange them when she's finished with what she's doing. "I can't believe I finally get to walk into this house and relax instead of picking up a hammer or a drill or a paint brush—"

"You're the one who was such a perfectionist about everything. If it had all been left up to me, I'd have kept it simple and had us in here at least three months ago."

"Huh, interesting, because as I recall, I said, 'hey, Pear, let's buy some land and build a house, so we can get exactly what we want,' and you said, 'or we could complicate the hell out of things and rebuild this old farmhouse I found instead.'"

"Oh, admit it. Every complication was worth it. And we did it. We saved this perfectly good house." She hops down off the stepladder and hands me a beer from the fridge. "But you can relax tomorrow. Right now, you need to light the grill. People will start showing up soon."

I take the beer and wrap my other hand around her waist, pulling her closer. "How much time do you think we have?"

"Not enough." She shakes her head at me, but those fuck-me eyes don't lie. She's thinking about it.

The front door swings open. No knock, no ring of the doorbell . . . and then the little intruder appears in the kitchen. "We're here!"

It's Tyson, Keller and Catie's youngest, who sees the stepladder Peri hasn't had a chance to put away as a conquest that can't be ignored. He's almost five, so I'm pretty sure he can handle three steps, but she puts her hands out to spot him, just in case.

"How are they early everywhere they go with five kids?" I set my beer down and head for the front door to greet our first guests.

"We only have four!" Keller yells as he walks through the door that his kid left standing wide open. I see his two older boys running for the backyard, no doubt hoping to find Crash, who is currently snoring on the couch.

Catie comes inside, carrying a dish covered in foil and Bella, who looks like she just woke up from a nap. "Well, for about seven more months, anyway."

"You're pregnant?" Peri yells from the kitchen. "Get in here!"

Our kitchen becomes a hub of hugs and congratulations.

The front door opens unannounced again, and Katie with a K's voice cuts through the celebration. "How long have y'all been hanging out without me?"

Three of Peri's friends from work trail in behind Katie and Derek. "Hold the door!" Lisa calls out to them, as if she can't just reopen it if they close it before she gets to it.

Maybe we should just prop the front door open and leave it that way, since it's obviously going to be opening and closing all day long.

"I don't own the damn electric company!" I yell, mostly as a joke, but also, I don't own the damn electric company!

"I drove two hours to your housewarming, little brother. You better be nice to me."

Lisa gives me a brief hug, and then runs to see what all the excitement's about in the kitchen.

My niece repeats her mom's routine, and then my nephew walks in, nods at the beer in my hand, and says, "Can I get one of those?"

His dad comes in behind him and slaps him in the back of the head. "No, but you can go find me one." I shake my brother-in-law's hand, tell him where to find the beer. He heads that way, his eyes taking in every detail of the finished house. He's making mental notes so he can give me a hard time later about how much money we spent restoring this place.

I close the door and hold onto the knob for a few beats. Peri was right.

Every complication was worth it.

Thank you for reading Peri. This book is a slight departure from my usual romantic comedies, though I hope you still found moments that made you laugh, sweat, and swoon. **AS A SPECIAL THANK YOU, I am offering a bonus scene** if you sign up for my newsletter. You can sign up from my website: https://indies-parks.net

For more laughs and steamy romance, please check out some of my other titles!

Steamy Rom-Com Duologies from INDIE SPARKS

VENGEFUL VIXENS:
Your Boss Says Hi!

She's only looking for a rebound guy, but her ex's boss plays for keeps. He's a former NFL player who used to have thousands of women screaming his name every week. Now, he only wants one woman to scream his name, and she just might become his biggest fan yet.

Your Trainer Says Hi!

She only wants to see her ex's beloved personal trainer in the gym—until he convinces her his hot tub could do wonders for her aching muscles. He isn't wrong, but between the heat, the bubbles, and his off-the-clock skills, she might be in too deep before she knows it. He's definitely not her type. So, why can't she stop seeing him?

NAUGHTY AT THE NOUVEAU:

Maintenance & Management

She's the new property manager. He's the new maintenance supervisor. They rub each other the wrong way . . . until they start to rub each other the right way. There's a non-fraternization policy, so they really shouldn't. But there's only one bed!

Landscaping & Leasing

He ghosted her after an unfortunate incident that she had absolutely no control over—and now, she's accidentally hired his landscaping company. She may not be completely immune to his charms (that voice!), but she's not weak enough to fall for him twice. But what if she doesn't know the whole story about why he disappeared from her life?

Stand-Alone Novellas

On My Merry Way

She may not have put "sexy stranger" on her Christmas list, but Santa knows what a good girl needs to make her holiday complete. Who knew one wrong-number text could turn out so right? Light the fireworks and pour the champagne! The naughty list is ready to make merry.

Modern Life of a Vintage Brat

She's an independent brat, who owns a vintage boutique. He's the smoking hot owner of the cigar bar next door, who is accustomed to being in control. She's not looking to be tamed, but she has no objection to him trying.